Defoe Abbott Hardy Marx Montaigne Machiavelli Chesterton Cooper Emerson Joyce Austen Hugo Eliot Grimm
Melville Haggard
Stoker Carroll Christie Maupassant Byron Molière Schiller
Wilde Engels Smith Kafka Hall Willis
Garnett Fitzgerald Einstein Hawthorne Dostoyevsky
Goethe Kipling Doyle
Cotton Henry Nietzsche
Baum Flaubert Turgenev Balzac
Leslie Dumas Stockton Vatsyayana Crane
Burroughs Verne
Curtis Tocqueville Whitman Gogol Vinci
Homer Widger Tolstoy Busch
Darwin Thoreau Twain Plato Scott Harte
Potter Freud Zola Lawrence Dickens Hesse
Kant Jowett Stevenson Burton
Andersen Cervantes
London Descartes Voltaire
Poe Aristotle Wells Cooke
Hale James Hastings
Bunner Shakespeare Irving
Richter Chekhov Chambers da Shaw Wodehouse
Doré Dante Swift Benedict Alcott
Pushkin
Newton

tredition

tredition was established in 2006 by Sandra Latusseck and Soenke Schulz. Based in Hamburg, Germany, tredition offers publishing solutions to authors and publishing houses, combined with world-wide distribution of printed and digital book content. tredition is uniquely positioned to enable authors and publishing houses to create books on their own terms and without conventional manu-facturing risks.

For more information please visit: www.tredition.com

TREDITION CLASSICS

This book is part of the TREDITION CLASSICS series. The creators of this series are united by passion for literature and driven by the intention of making all public domain books available in printed format again - worldwide. Most TREDITION CLASSICS titles have been out of print and off the bookstore shelves for decades. At tredition we believe that a great book never goes out of style and that its value is eternal. Several mostly non-profit literature projects provide content to tredition. To support their good work, tredition donates a portion of the proceeds from each sold copy. As a reader of a TREDITION CLASSICS book, you support our mission to save many of the amazing works of world literature from oblivion. See all available books at www.tredition.com.

 Project Gutenberg

The content for this book has been graciously provided by Project Gutenberg. Project Gutenberg is a non-profit organization founded by Michael Hart in 1971 at the University of Illinois. The mission of Project Gutenberg is simple: To encourage the creation and distribution of eBooks. Project Gutenberg is the first and largest collection of public domain eBooks.

Yorkshire Ditties, Second Series To which is added The Cream of Wit and Humour from his Popular Writings

John Hartley

Imprint

This book is part of TREDITION CLASSICS

Author: John Hartley
Cover design: Buchgut, Berlin – Germany

Publisher: tredition GmbH, Hamburg - Germany
ISBN: 978-3-8424-8520-4

www.tredition.com
www.tredition.de

Copyright:
The content of this book is sourced from the public domain.

The intention of the TREDITION CLASSICS series is to make world literature in the public domain available in printed format. Literary enthusiasts and organizations, such as Project Gutenberg, worldwide have scanned and digitally edited the original texts. tredition has subsequently formatted and redesigned the content into a modern reading layout. Therefore, we cannot guarantee the exact reproduction of the original format of a particular historic edition. Please also note that no modifications have been made to the spelling, therefore it may differ from the orthography used today.

DEDICATION.

To RICHARD CHERRY, C. E.,

as a small token of the respect in which he is
held by The Author.

PREFACE.

We offer no apology for presenting this little book to the public, feeling sure from our past experience, that it will be kindly welcomed by a great many lovers of their "native twang."
THE PUBLISHERS.

CONTENTS of Second Series.

Moral.

Rejected.

Duffin Johnie.

Lost Love.

Th' Traitle Sop.

To Let.

Fault Finders.

Disapointment.

Work Away.

New Machinery &c.

September Month.

A Hawporth.

Buttermilk &c.

It's a comfort.

Progress.

Try Again.

Jealousy.

Winter.

Persevere.

Booith-Taan Election.

Election.

None think Alike.

Seaside.

Th' Better Part.

A poor owd man wi' tott'ring gait,
Wi' body bent, and snowy pate,
Aw met one day;—
An' daan o' th' rooad side grassy banks
He sat to rest his weary shanks;
An' aw, to wile away my time,
O'th' neighbouring hillock did recline,
An' bade "gooid day."

Said aw, "Owd friend, pray tell me true,
If in your heart yo niver rue
The time 'ats past?
Does envy niver fill your breast
When passin fowk wi' riches blest?
An' do yo niver think it wrang
At yo should have to trudge alang,
Soa poor to th' last?"

"Young man," he said "aw envy nooan;
But ther are times aw pity some,
Wi' all mi heart;
To see what troubled lives they spend,
What cares upon their hands depend;
Then aw in thoughtfulness declare
'At 'little cattle little care'
Is th' better part.

Gold is a burden hard to carry,
An' tho' Dame Fortune has been chary
O' gifts to me;
Yet still aw strive to feel content,
An' think what is, for th' best is meant;
An' th' mooast ov all aw strive for here,
Is still to keep mi conscience clear,
From dark spots free.

An' while some tax ther brains to find
What they'll be forced to leave behind,

When th' time shall come;
Aw try bi honest word an' deed,
To get what little here aw need,
An' live i' hopes at last to say,
When breath go as flickerin away,
'Awm gooin hooam.'"

Aw gave his hand a hearty shake,
It seem'd as tho' the words he spake
Sank i' mi heart:
Aw walk'd away a wiser man,
Detarmined aw wod try his plan
I' hopes at last 'at aw might be
As weel assured ov Heaven as he;
That's th' better part.

Done Agean.

Aw've a rare lump o' beef on a dish,
We've some bacon 'at's hung up o' th' thack,
We've as mich gooid spike-cake as we wish,
An' wi' currens its varry near black;
We've a barrel o' gooid hooam brewed drink,
We've a pack o' flaar reared agean th' clock,
We've a load o' puttates under th' sink,
So we're pretty weel off as to jock.
Aw'm soa fain aw can't tell whear to bide,
But the cause aw dar hardly let aat;
It suits me moor nor all else beside;
Aw've a paand 'at th' wife knows nowt abaat.

Aw can nah have a spree to misel?
Aw can treat mi old mates wi' a glass;
An' aw sha'nt ha' to come home an' tell
My old lass, ha' aw've shut all mi brass.
Some fowk say, when a chap's getten wed,
He should nivver keep owt thro' his wife;
If he does awve oft heard 'at it's sed,
'At it's sure to breed trouble an' strife;
If it does aw'm net baan to throw up,

Tho' aw'd mich rayther get on withaat;
But who wodn't risk a blow up,
For a paand 'at th' wife knows nowt abaat.

Aw hid it i' th' coil hoil last neet,
For fear it dropt aat o' mi fob,
Coss aw knew, if shoo happened to see 't,
At mi frolic wod prove a done job.
But aw'll gladden mi een wi' its face,
To mak sure at its safe in its nick; —
But aw'm blest if ther's owt left i' th' place!
Why, its hook'd it as sure as aw'm wick.
Whear its gooan to's a puzzle to me,
An' who's taen it aw connot mak aat,
For it connot be th' wife, coss you see
It's a paand 'at shoo knew nowt abaat.

But thear shoo is, peepin' off th' side,
An' aw see'at shoo's all on a grin;
To chait her aw've monny a time tried,
But I think it's nah time to give in.
A chap may be deep as a well,
But a woman's his maister when done;
He may chuckle and flatter hissel,
But he'll wakken to find at shoo's won.
It's a rayther unpleasant affair,
Yet it's better it's happened noa daat;
Aw'st be fain to come in for a share
O' that paand at th' wife knows all abaat.

Latter Wit.

Awm sittin o' that old stooan seeat,
Wheear last aw set wi' thee;
It seems long years sin' last we met,
Awm sure it must be three.

Awm wond'rin what aw sed or did,
Or what aw left undone:

'At made thi hook it, an' get wed,
To one tha used to shun.

Aw dooant say awm a handsom chap,
Becoss aw know awm net;
But if aw wor 'ith' mind to change,
He isn't th' chap, aw'll bet.

Awm net a scoller, but aw know
A long chawk moor ner him;
It couldn't be his knowledge box
'At made thi change thi whim.

He doesn't haddle as mich brass
As aw do ivery wick:
An' if he gets a gradely shop,
It's seldom he can stick.

An' then agean,—he goes on th' rant;
Nah, that aw niver do;—
Aw allus mark misen content,
Wi' an odd pint or two.

His brother is a lazy lout,—
His sister's nooan too gooid,—
Ther's net a daycent 'en ith' bunch,—
Vice seems to run ith' blooid.

An yet th'art happy,—soa they say,
That caps me moor ner owt!
Tha taks a deal less suitin, lass,
Nor iver awst ha' thowt.

Aw saw yo walkin aat one neet,
Befoor yo'd getten wed;
Aw guess'd what he wor tawkin, tho
Aw dooant know what he sed.

But he'd his arm araand thi waist,

An tho' thi face wor hid,
Aw'll swear aw saw him kuss thi:—
That's what aw niver did.

Aw thowt tha'd order him away,
An' mak a fearful row,
But tha niver tuk noa nooatice,
Just as if tha didn't know.

Awm hawf inclined to think sometimes,
Aw've been a trifle soft,
Aw happen should a' dun't misen?
Aw've lang'd to do it oft.

Thar't lost to me, but if a chonce
Should turn up by-an-by,
If aw get seck'd aw'll bet me booits,
That isn't t'reason why.

My Gronfayther's Days.

A'a, Jonny! a'a Johnny! aw'm sooary for thee!
But come thi ways to me, an' sit o' mi knee,
For it's shockin' to hearken to th' words 'at tha says:—
Ther wor nooan sich like things i' thi gronofayther's days.

When aw wor a lad, lads wor lads, tha knows, then,
But nahdays they owt to be 'shamed o' thersen;
For they smook, an' they drink, an' get other bad ways;
Things wor different once i' thi gronfayther's days.

Aw remember th' furst day aw went a coortin' a bit,
An' walked aght thi granny;—awst niver forget;
For we blushed wol us faces wor all in a blaze;—
It wor nooa sin to blush i' thi gronfayther's days.

Ther's nooa lasses nah, John, 'at's fit to be wed;
They've false teeth i' ther maath, an false hair o' ther heead;
They're a make up o' buckram, an' waddin', an' stays,
But a lass wor a lass i' thi gronfayther's days.

At that time a tradesman dealt fairly wi' th' poor,
But nah a fair dealer can't keep oppen th' door;
He's a fooil if he fails, he's a scamp if he pays;
Ther wor honest men lived i' thi gronfayther's days.

Ther's chimleys an' factrys i' ivery nook nah,
But ther's varry few left 'at con fodder a caah;
An' ther's telegraff poles all o'th edge o'th' highways,
Whear grew bonny green trees i' thi gronfayther's days.

We're teld to be thankful for blessin's at's sent,
An' aw hooap 'at tha'll allus be blessed wi' content;
Tha mun make th' best tha con o' this world wol tha stays,
But aw wish tha'd been born i' thi gronfayther's days.

Heart Brocken.

He wor a poor hard workin lad,
An' shoo a workin lass:
An' hard they tew'd throo day to day,
For varry little brass.
An' oft they tawk'd o'th' weddin' day,
An' lang'd for th' happy time,
When poverty noa moor should part,
Two lovers i' ther prime.

But wark wor scarce, an' wages low
An' mait an' drink wor dear,
They did ther best to struggle on,
As year crept after year.
But they wor little better off,
Nor what they'd been befoor;
It tuk 'em all ther time to keep
Grim Want aatside 'oth' door.

Soa things went on, wol Hope at last,
Gave place to dark despair;
They felt they'd nowt but lovin hearts,
An' want an toil to share.
At length he screw'd his courage up

To leave his native shore;
An' goa where wealth wor worshipped less,
An' men wor valued moor.

He towld his tale;—poor lass!—a tear
Just glistened in her e'e;
Then soft shoo whispered, "please thisen,
But think sometimes o' me:
An' whether tha's gooid luck or ill,
Tha knows aw shall be glad
To see thee safe at hooam agean,
An' welcome back mi lad."

"Awl labor on, an' do mi best;
Tho' lonely aw must feel,
But awst be happy an content
If tha be dooin weel.
But ne'er forget tho' waves may roll,
An' keep us far apart;
Thas left a poor, poor lass behind,
An taen away her heart."

"Dost think 'at aw can e'er forget,
Wheariver aw may rooam,
That bonny face an' lovin heart,
Awve prized soa dear at hoam?
Nay lass, nooan soa, be sure o' this,
'At till next time we meet
Tha'll be mi first thowt ivery morn,
An' last thowt ivery neet."

He went a way an' years flew by,
But tidins seldom came;
Shoo couldn't help, at times, a sigh,
But breathed noa word o' blame;
When one fine day a letter came,
'Twor browt to her at th' mill,
Shoo read it, an' her tremlin bands,
An' beating heart stood still.

Her fellow workers gathered raand
An caught her as shoo fell,
An' as her heead droop'd o' ther arms,
Shoo sighed a sad "farewell.
Poor lass! her love had proved untrue,
He'd play'd a traitor's part,
He'd taen another for his bride,
An' broke a trustin heart."

Her doleful story sooin wor known,
An' monny a tear wor shed;
They took her hooam an' had her laid,
Upon her humble bed;
Shoo'd nawther kith nor kin to come
Her burial fees to pay;
But some poor comrade's undertuk,
To see her put away.

Each gave what little helps they could,
From aat ther scanty stoor;
I' hopes 'at some at roll'd i' wealth
Wod give a trifle moor.
But th' maisters ordered 'em away,
Abaat ther business, sharp!
For shoo'd deed withaat a nooatice,
An' shoo hadn't fell'd her warp.

To a Daisy,

Found blooming March 7th.

A'a awm feeared tha's come too sooin,
Little daisy!
Pray, whativer wor ta doin?
Are ta crazy?
Winter winds are blowin' yet,

Tha'll be starved, mi little pet.

Did a gleam'o' sunshine warm thee,
An deceive thee?
Niver let appearance charm thee,
For believe me,
Smiles tha'll find are oft but snares,
Laid to catch thee unawares.

Still aw think it luks a shame,
To tawk sich stuff;
Aw've lost faith, an tha'll do th' same,
Hi, sooin enuff:
If tha'rt happy as tha art
Trustin' must be th' wisest part.

Come, aw'll pile some bits o' stooan,
Raand thi dwellin';
They may screen thee when aw've gooan
Ther's no tellin';
An' when gentle spring draws near
Aw'll release thee, niver fear.

An' if then thi pratty face,
Greets me smilin';
Aw may come an' sit bith' place,
Time beguilin';
Glad to think aw'd paar to be,
Ov some use, if but to thee.

A Bad Sooart.

Aw'd raythur face a redwut brick,
Sent flyin' at mi heead;
Aw'd raythur track a madman's steps,
Whearivei they may leead;
Aw'd raythur ventur in a den,
An' stail a lion's cub:
Aw'd raythur risk the foamin wave

In an old leaky tub;
Aw'd raythur stand i'th' midst o'th fray,
Whear bullets thickest shower;
Nor trust a mean, black hearted man,
At's th' luck to be i' power.

A redwut brick may miss its mark,
A madman change his whim;
A lion may forgive a theft;
A leaky tub may swim;
Bullets may pass yo harmless by,
An' leave all safe at last;
A thaasand thunders shake the sky,
An' spare yo when they've past;
Yo' may o'ercome mooast fell disease;
Make poverty yo'r friend;
But wi' a mean, blackhearted man,
Noa mortal can contend.

Ther's malice in his kindest smile,
His proffered hand's a snare;
He's plannin deepest villany,
When seemingly mooast fair;
He leads yo' on wi' oily tongue,
Swears he's yo're fastest friend.
He get's yo' once within his coils,
An' crushes yo' ith' end.
Old Nick, we're tell'd, gooas prowlin' aat,
An' seeks whom to devour;
But he's a saint, compared to some,
'At's th' luk to be i' power.

All we Had.

It worn't for her winnin ways,
Nor for her bonny face
But shoo wor th' only lass we had,
An that quite alters th' case.

We'd two fine lads as yo need see,

An' weel we love 'em still;
But shoo war th' only lass we had,
An' we could spare her ill.

We call'd her bi mi mother's name,
It saanded sweet to me;
We little thowt ha varry sooin
Awr pet wod have to dee.

Aw used to watch her ivery day,
Just like a oppenin bud;
An' if aw couldn't see her change,
Aw fancied' at aw could.

Throo morn to neet her little tongue
Wor allus on a stir;
Awve heeard a deeal o' childer lisp,
But nooan at lispt like her.

Sho used to play all sooarts o' tricks,
'At childer shouldn't play;
But then, they wor soa nicely done,
We let her have her way.

But bit bi bit her spirits fell,
Her face grew pale an' thin;
For all her little fav'rite toys
Shoo didn't care a pin.

Aw saw th' old wimmin shak ther heeads,
Wi monny a doleful nod;
Aw knew they thowt shoo'd goa, but still
Aw couldn't think shoo wod.

Day after day my wife an' me,
Bent o'er that suff'rin child,
Shoo luk'd at mammy, an' at me,
Then shut her een an' smiled.

At last her spirit pass'd away;
Her once breet een wor dim;
Shoo'd heeard her Maker whisper 'come,'
An' hurried off to Him.

Fowk tell'd us t'wor a sin to grieve,
For God's will must be best;
But when yo've lost a child yo've loved,
It puts yor Faith to th' test.

We pick'd a little bit o' graand,
Whear grass and daisies grew,
An' trees wi spreeadin boughs aboon
Ther solemn shadows threw.

We saw her laid to rest, within
That deep grave newly made;
Wol th' sexton let a tear drop fall,
On th' handle ov his spade.

It troubled us to walk away,
An' leeav her bi hersen;
Th' full weight o' what we'd had to bide,
We'd niver felt till then.

But th' hardest task wor yet to come,
That pang can ne'er be towld;
'Twor when aw feszend th' door at nee't,
An' locked her aat i'th' cowld.

'Twor then hot tears roll'd daan mi cheek,
'Twor then aw felt mooast sad;
For shoo'd been sich a tender plant,
An' th' only lass we had.

But nah we're growin moor resign'd,
Although her face we miss;
For He's blest us wi another,
An we've hopes o' rearin this,

Give it 'em Hot.

Give it 'em hot, an be hanged to ther feelins!
Souls may be lost wol yor choosin' yor words!
Out wi' them doctrines 'at taich o' fair dealins!
Daan wi' a vice tho' it may be a lord's!
What does it matter if truth be unpleasant?
Are we to lie a man's pride to exalt!
Why should a prince be excused, when a peasant
Is bullied an' blamed for a mich smaller fault?

O, ther's too mich o' that sneakin and bendin;
An honest man still should be fearless and bold;
But at this day fowk seem to be feeared ov offendin,
An' they'll bow to a cauf if it's nobbut o' gold.
Give me a crust tho' it's dry, an' a hard 'en,
If aw know it's my own aw can ait it wi' glee;
Aw'd rayther bith hauf work all th' day for a farden,
Nor haddle a fortun wi' bendin' mi knee.

Let ivery man by his merit be tested,
Net by his pocket or th' clooas on his back;
Let hypocrites all o' ther clooaks be divested,
An' what they're entitled to, that let em tak.
Give it 'em hot! but remember when praichin,
All yo 'at profess others failins to tell,
'At yo'll do far moor gooid wi' yor tawkin an' taichin,
If yo set an example, an' improve yorsel.

Th' Honest Hard Worker.

It's hard what poor fowk mun put u'p wi'!
What insults an' snubs they've to tak!
What bowin an' scrapin's expected,
If a chap's a black coit on his back.
As if clooas made a chap ony better,
Or riches improved a man's heart,
As if muck in a carriage smell'd sweeter
Nor th' same muck wod smell in a cart.

Give me one, hard workin, an' honest,
Tho' his clooas may be greasy and coorse;
If it's muck 'ats been getten bi labor,
It does'nt mak th' man ony worse.
Awm sick o' thease simpering dandies,
'At think coss they've getten some brass,
They've a reight to luk daan at th' hard workers,
An' curl up their nooas as they pass.

It's a poor sooart o' life to be leadin,
To be curlin an' partin ther hair;
An' seekin one's own fun and pleasure,
Niver thinkin ha others mun fare.
It's all varry weel to be spendin
Ther time at a hunt or a ball,
But if th' workers war huntin an' doncin,
Whativer wad come on us all?

Ther's summat beside fun an' frolic
To live for, aw think, if we try;
Th' world owes moor to a honest hard worker
Nor it does to a rich fly-bi-sky.
Tho' wealth aw acknowledge is useful,
An' awve oft felt a want on't misen,
Yet th' world withaat brass could keep movin,
But it wodn't do long withaat men.

One truth they may put i' ther meersham,
An' smoke it — that is if they can;
A man may mak hooshuns o' riches,
But riches can ne'er mak a man.
Then give me that honest hard worker,
'At labors throo marnin to neet,
Tho' his rest may be little an' seldom,
Yet th' little he gets he finds sweet.

He may rank wi' his wealthier brother,
An' rank heigher, aw fancy, nor some;

For a hand 'at's weel hoofed wi' hard labor
Is a passport to th' world 'at's to come.
For we know it's a sin to be idle,
As man's days i' this world are but few;
Then let's all wi' awr lot 'be contented,
An' continue to toil an' to tew.

For ther's one thing we all may be sure on,
If we each do awr best wol we're here,
'At when, th' time comes for reckonin, we're called on,
We shall have varry little to fear.
An' at last, when, we throw daan awr tackle,
An' are biddin farewell to life's stage,
May we hear a voice whisper at partin,
"Come on, lad! Tha's haddled thi wage;"

Niver Heed.

Let others boast ther bit o' brass,
That's moor nor aw can do;
Aw'm nobbut one o'th' working class,
'At's strugglin to pool throo;
An' if it's little 'at aw get,
It's littie 'at aw need;
An' if sometimes aw'm pinched a bit,
Aw try to niver heed.

Some fowk they tawk o' brokken hearts,
An' mourn ther sorry fate,
Becoss they can't keep sarvent men,
An' dine off silver plate;
Aw think they'd show more gradely wit
To listen to my creed,
An' things they find they cannot get,
Why, try to niver heed.

Ther's some 'at lang for parks an' halls,
An' letters to ther name;
But happiness despises walls,

It's nooan a child o' fame.
A robe may lap a woeful chap,
Whose heart wi grief may bleed,
Wol rags may rest on joyful breast,
Soa hang it! niver heed!

Th' sun shines as breet for me as them,
An' th' meadows smell as sweet,
Th' larks sing as sweetly o'er mi heead,
An' th' flaars smile at mi feet,
An' when a hard day's wark is done,
Aw ait mi humble feed,
Mi appetite's a relish fun,
Soa hang it, niver heed.

Sing On.

Sing on, tha bonny burd, sing on, sing on;
Aw cannot sing;
A claad hings ovver me, do what aw con
Fresh troubles spring.
Aw wish aw could, like thee, fly far away,
Aw'd leave mi cares an be a burd to-day.
Mi heart war once as full o' joy as thine,
But nah it's sad;
Aw thowt all th' happiness i'th' world wor mine,
Sich faith aw had; —
But he who promised aw should be his wife
Has robb'd me o' mi ivery joy i' life.
Sing on: tha cannot cheer me wi' thi song;
Yet, when aw hear
Thi warblin' voice, 'at rings soa sweet an' strong,
Aw feel a tear
Roll daan mi cheek, 'at gives mi heart relief,
A gleam o' comfort, but it's varry brief.
This little darlin', cuddled to mi breast,
It little knows,
When snoozlin' soa quietly at rest,
'At all mi woes

Are smothered thear, an' mi poor heart ud braik
But just aw live for mi wee laddie's sake.
Sing on; an' if tha e'er should chonce to see
That faithless swain,
Whose falsehood has caused all mi misery,
Strike up thy strain,
An' if his heart yet answers to thy trill
Fly back to me, an' aw will love him still.
But if he heeds thee not, then shall aw feel
All hope is o'er,
An' he that aw believed an' loved soa weel
Be loved noa more;
For that hard heart, bird music cannot move,
Is far too cold a dwellin'-place for love.

What aw Want.

Gie me a little humble cot,
A bit o' garden graand,
Set in some quiet an' sheltered spot,
Wi' hills an' trees all raand;

An' if besides mi hooam ther flows
A little mumuring rill,
At sings sweet music as it gooas,
Awst like it better still.

Gie me a wife 'at loves me weel,
An' childer two or three,
Wi' health to sweeten ivery meal,
An' hearts brimful o' glee.

Gie me a chonce, wi' honest toil
Mi efforts to engage,
Gie me a maister who can smile
When forkin aght mi wage.

Gie me a friend 'at aw can trust,
'An tell mi secrets to;

One tender-hearted, firm an' just,
Who sticks to what is true.

Gie me a pipe to smook at neet,
A pint o' hooam-brew'd ale,
A faithful dog 'at runs to meet
Me wi a waggin tail.

A cat to purr o'th' fender rims,
To freeten th' mice away;
A cosy bed to rest mi limbs
Throo neet to commin day.

Gie me all this, an' aw shall be
Content, withaat a daat,
But if denied, then let me be
Content to live withaat.

For 'tisn't th' wealth one may possess
Can purchase pleasures true;
For he's th' best chonce o' happiness,
Whose wants are small an' few.

What it is to be Mother.

A'a, dear! what a life has a mother!
At leeast, if they're hamper'd like me,
Thro' mornin' to neet ther's some bother,
An' ther will be, aw guess, wol aw dee.

Ther's mi chap, an misen, an' six childer,
Six o'th' roughest, aw think, under th' sun,
Aw'm sartin sometimes they'd bewilder
Old Joab, wol his patience wor done.

They're i' mischief i' ivery corner,
An' ther tongues they seem niver at rest;
Ther's one shaatin' "Little Jack Horner,"
An' another "The realms o' the blest."

Aw'm sure if a body's to watch 'em,
They mun have een at th' back o' ther yed;
For quiet yo niver can catch 'em
Unless they're asleep an' i' bed.

For ther's somdy comes runnin to tell us
'At one on em's takken wi' fits;
Or ther's two on 'em feightin for th' bellus,
An' rivin' ther clooas all i' bits.

In a mornin' they're all weshed an' tidy'd,
But bi nooin they're as black as mi shoe;
To keep a lot cleean, if yo've tried it,
Yo know 'at ther's summat to do.

When my felly comes hooam to his drinkin',
Aw try to be gradely, an' straight;
For when all's nice an' cleean, to mi thinkin',
He enjoys better what ther's to ait.

If aw tell him aw'm varry near finished
Wi allus been kept in a fuss,
He says, as he looks up astonished,
"Why, aw niver see owt 'at tha does."

But aw wonder who does all ther mendin',
Weshes th' clooas, an cleans th' winders an' flags?
But for me they'd have noa spot to stand in —
They'd be lost i' ther filth an' ther rags.

But it allus wor soa, an' it will be,
A chap thinks' at a woman does nowt;
But it ne'er bothers me what they tell me,
For men havn't a morsel o' thowt.

But just harken to me wol aw'm tellin'
Ha aw tew to keep ivery thing straight;
An' aw'l have yo for th' judge if yor willin',

For aw want nowt but what aw think's reight.

Ov a Monday aw start o' my weshin',
An' if th' day's fine aw get um all dried;
Ov a Tuesday aw fettle mi kitchen,
An' mangle, an' iron beside.

Ov a Wednesday, then aw've mi bakin';
Ov a Thursday aw reckon to brew;
Ov a Friday all th' carpets want shakin',
An' aw've th' bedrooms to clean an' dust throo.

Then o'th' Setterday, after mi markets,
Stitch on buttons, an' th' stockins' to mend,
Then aw've all th' Sundy clooas to luk ovver,
An' that brings a week's wark to its end.

Then o'th' Sundy ther's cooking 'em th' dinner,
It's ther only warm meal in a wick;
Tho' ther's some say aw must be a sinner,
For it's paving mi way to Old Nick.

But a chap mun be like to ha' summat,
An' aw can't think it's varry far wrang,
Just to cook him an' th' childer a dinner,
Tho' it may mak me rayther too thrang.

But if yor a wife an' a mother,
Yo've yor wark an' yor duties to mind;
Yo mun leearn to tak nowt as a bother,
An' to yor own comforts be blind.

But still, just to seer all ther places,
When they're gethred raand th' harston at neet,
Fill'd wi six roosy-red, smilin' faces;
It's nooan a despisable seet.

An, aw connot help thinkin' an' sayin',
(Tho' yo may wonder what aw can mean),

'At if single, aw sooin should be playin'
Coortin tricks, an' be weddin' agean.

What is It.

What is it maks a crusty wife
Forget to scold, an' leeave off strife?
What is it smoothes the rooad throo life?
It's sooap.

What is it maks a gaumless muff
Grow rich, an' roll i' lots o' stuff,
Woll better men can't get enough?
It's sooap.

What is it, if it worn't theear,
Wod mak some fowk feel varry queer,
An' put 'em: i' ther proper sphere?
It's sooap.

What is' it maks fowk wade throo th' snow,
To goa to th' church, becoss they know
'At th' squire's at hooam an' sure to goa?
It's sooap.

What is it gains fowk invitations,
Throo them 'at live i' lofty stations?
What is it wins mooast situations?
It's sooap.

What is it men say they detest,
Yet alus like that chap the best
'At gives 'em twice as mich as th' rest?
It's sooap.

What is it, when the devil sends
His agents raand to work his ends,
What is it gains him lots o' friends?
It's sooap.

What is it we should mooast despise,
An' by its help refuse to rise,

Tho' poverty's befoor awr eyes?
It's sooap.

What is it, when life's wastin' fast,
When all this world's desires are past,
Will prove noa use to us at last?
It's sooap.

Come thi Ways!

Bonny lassie, come thi ways,
An' let us goa together!
Tho' we've met wi stormy days,
Ther'll be some sunny weather:
An' if joy should spring for me,
Tha shall freely share it;
An' if trouble comes to thee,
Aw can help to bear it.

Tho thi mammy says us nay,
An' thi dad's unwillin';
Wod ta have me pine away
Wi' this love 'at's killin'?
Come thi ways, an' let me twine
Mi arms once moor abaght thee;
Weel tha knows mi heart is thine,
Aw couldn't live withaat thee.

Ivery day an' haar 'at slips,
Some pleasure we are missin',
For those bonny rooasy lips
Aw'm niver stall'd o' kissin',
If men wor wise to walk life's track
Withaat sith joys to glad 'em,
He must ha' made a sad mistak
'At gave a Eve to Adam.

Advice to Jenny.

Jenny, Jenny, dry thi ee,
An' dunnot luk soa sad;
It grieves me varry mich to see
Tha freeats abaat yon lad;
For weel tha knows, withaat a daat,
Wheariver he may be,
Tho fond o' rammellin' abaat,
He's allus true to thee.

Tha'll learn mooar sense, lass, in a while,
For wisdom comes wi' time,
An' if tha lives tha'll leearn to smile
At troubles sich as thine;
A faithful chap is better far,
Altho' he likes to rooam,
Nor one 'at does what isn't reight,
An' sits o'th' hearth at hooam.

Tha needn't think 'at wedded life
Noa disappointment brings;
Tha munnot think to keep a chap
Teed to thi appron strings:
Soa dry thi een, they're varry wet,
An' let thi heart be glad,
For tho' tha's wed a rooamer, yet,
Tha's wed a honest lad.

Ther's mony a lady, rich an' great,
'At's sarvents at her call,
Wod freely change her grand estate
For thine tha thinks soa small:
For riches cannot buy content,
Soa tho' thi joys be few,
Tha's one ther's nowt con stand anent,—
A heart 'at's kind an' true.

Soa when he comes luk breet an' gay,

An' meet him wi' a kiss,
Tha'll find him mooar inclined to stay
Wi treatment sich as this;
But if thi een luk red like that,
He'll see all's wrang at once,
He'll leet his pipe, an' don his hat,
An' bolt if he's a chonce.

Ther's mich Expected.

Life's pathway is full o' deep ruts,
An' we mun tak gooid heed lest we stumble;
Man is made up of "ifs" and of "buts,"
It'seems pairt ov his natur to grumble.

But if we'd anxiously tak
To makkin' things smooth as we're able,
Ther'd be monny a better clooath'd back,
An' monny a better spread table.

It's a sad state o' things when a man
Connot put ony faith in his brother,
An' fancies he'll chait if he can,
An' rejoice ovver th' fall ov another.

An' it's sad when yo see some 'at stand
High in social position an' power,
To know at ther fortuns wor plann'd
An' built, aght o'th' wrecks o' those lower.

It's sad to see luxury rife,
An' fortuns being thowtlessly wasted;
While others are wearin' aat life,
With the furst drops o' pleasure untasted.

Some in carriages rollin' away,
To a ball, or a rout, or a revel;
But their chariots may bear 'em some day
Varry near to the gates ov the devil.

Oh! charity surely is rare,
Or ther'd net be soa monny neglected;
For ther's lots wi enuff an' to spare,
An' from them varry mich is expected.

An' tho' in this world they've ther fill
Of its pleasures, an' wilfully blinded,
Let deeath come—as surely it will—
They'll be then ov ther duties reminded.

An' when called on, they, tremblin' wi' fear,
Say "The hungry an' nak'd we ne'er knew,"
That sentence shall fall on their ear—
"Depart from me; I never knew you."

Then, oh! let us do what we can,
Nor with this world's goods play the miser;
If it's wise to lend money to man,
To lend to the Lord must be wiser.

A Strange Stooary.

Aw know some fowk will call it crime,
To put sich stooaries into ryhme,
But yet, contentedly aw chime
Mi simple ditty:
An if it's all a waste o' time,
The moor's the pity.

— — —

O'er Wibsey Slack aw coom last neet,
Wi' reekin heead and weary feet,
A strange, strange chap, aw chonced to meet;
He made mi start;
But pluckin up, aw did him greet
Wi beatin heart.

His dress wor black as black could be,
An th' latest fashion aw could see,

But yet they hung soa dawderly,
Like suits i' shops;
Bith heart! yo mud ha putten three
Sich legs i'th' slops.

Says aw, "Owd trump, it's rather late
For one at's dress'd i' sich a state,
Across this Slack to mak ther gate:
Is ther some pairty?
Or does ta allus dress that rate —
Black duds o'th' wairty?"

He twisted raand as if to see
What sooart o' covy aw cud be,
An' grinned wi sich a maath at me,
It threw me sick!
"Lor saves!" aw cried, "an' is it thee
At's call'd ow'd Nick!"

But when aw luk'd up into th' place,
Whear yo'd expect to find a face;
A awful craytur met mi gaze,
It took mi puff:
"Gooid chap," aw sed, "please let me pass,
Aw've seen enough!"

Then bendin cloise daan to mi ear,
He tell'd me 'at aw'd nowt to fear,
An' soa aw stop't a bit to hear
What things he'd ax;
But as he spake his, teeth rang clear,
Like knick-a-nacks.

"A'a, Jack," he sed, "aw'm capt 'wi thee
Net knowin sich a chap as me;
For oft when tha's been on a spree,
Aw've been thear too;
But tho' aw've reckon'd safe o' thee,
Tha's just edged throo.

Mi name is Deeath — tha needn't start,
And put thi hand upon thi heart,

For tha ma see 'at aw've noa dart
Wi which to strike;
Let's sit an' tawk afoor we part,
O'th edge o'th dyke."

"Nay, nay, that tale weant do, owd lad,
For Bobby Burns tells me tha had
A scythe hung o'er thi' shoulder, Gad!
Tha worn't dress'd
I' fine black clooath; tha wore' a plad
Across thi breast!"

"Well, Jack," he said, "thar't capt no daat
To find me' wanderin abaght;
But th' fact is, lad, 'at aw'm withaat
A job to do;
Mi scythe aw've had to put up th' spaat,
Mi arrows too."

"Yo dunnot mean to tell to me,
'At fowk noa moor will ha' to dee?"
"Noa, hark a minit an' tha'll see
When th' truth aw tell!
Fowk do withaat mi darts an me,
Thev kill thersel.

They do it too at sich a rate
Wol mi owd system's aght o' date;
What we call folly, they call fate;
An' all ther pleasur
Is ha' to bring ther life's estate
To th' shortest measur.

They waste ther time, an' waste ther gains,
O' stuff 'at's brew'd throo poisoned grains,
Thro' morn to neet they keep ther brains,
For ever swimmin,
An' if a bit o' sense remains,
It's fun i'th wimmen.

Tha'll find noa doctors wi ther craft,
Nor yet mysen wi scythe or shaft,

E'er made as monny deead or daft,
As Gin an' Rum,
An' if aw've warn'd fowk, then they've lafft
At me, bi gum!

But if they thus goa on to swill,
They'll not want Wilfrid Lawson's bill,
For give a druffen chap his fill,
An sooin off pops he,
An teetotal fowk moor surely still,
Will dee wi th' dropsy.

It's a queer thing at sich a nation
Can't use a bit o' moderation;
But one lot rush to ther damnation
Through love o'th bottle:
Wol others think to win salvation
Wi being teetotal."

Wi' booany neive he stroked mi heead,
"Tak my advice, young chap," he sed,
"Let liquors be, sup ale asteead,
An' tha'll be better,
An' dunnot treat th' advice tha's heard
Like a dead letter."

"Why Deeath," aw sed, "fowk allus say,
Yo come to fotch us chaps away!
But this seems strange, soa tell me pray,
Ha wor't yo coom?
Wor it to tell us keep away,
Yo hav'nt room?"

"Stop whear tha art, Jack, if tha dar
But tha'll find spirits worse bi far
Sarved aght i' monny a public bar,
At's thowt quite lawful;
Nor what tha'll find i'th' places par-
Sons call soa awful."

"Gooid bye!" he sed, an' off he shot,
Leavin behind him sich a lot

O' smook, as blue as it wor hot!
It set me stewin!
Soa hooam aw cut, an' gate a pot
Ov us own brewin.

— — — —

If when yo've read this stooary through,
Yo daat if it's exactly true,
Yo'll nobbut do as others do,
Yo may depend on't.
Blow me! aw ommost daat it too,
So thear's an end on't

Take Heart.

Roughest roads, we often find,
Lead us on to th' nicest places;
Kindest hearts oft hide behind
Some o'th' plainest-lukkin faces.

Flaars' whose colors breetest are,
Oft delight awr wond'ring seet;
But thers others, humbler far,
Smell a thaasand times as sweet.

Burds o' monny color'd feather,
Please us as they skim along,
But ther charms all put together,
Connot equal th' skylark's song.

Bonny women — angels seemin, —
Set awr hearts an' brains o' fire;
But its net ther beauties; beamin,
Its ther gooidness we admire.

Th' bravest man 'at's in a battle,
Isn't allus th' furst i'th' fray;
He best proves his might an' mettle,
Who remains to win the day.

Monkey's an' vain magpies chatter,
But it doesn't prove em wise;
An it's net wi noise an' clatter,
Men o' sense expect to rise.

'Tisn't them 'at promise freely,
Are mooast ready to fulfill;
An' 'tisn't them 'at trudge on dreely
'At are last at top o'th' hill.

Bad hauf-craans may pass as payment,
Gaudy flaars awr een beguile;
Women may be loved for raiment,
Show may blind us for a while;

But we sooin grow discontented,
An' for solid worth we sigh,
An' we leearn to prize the jewel,
Tho it's hidden from the eye.

Him 'at thinks to gether diamonds
As he walks along his rooad,
Niver need be tired wi' huggin,
For he'll have a little looad.

Owt 'at's worth a body's winnin
Mun be toiled for long an' hard;
An' tho' th' struggle may be pinnin,
Perseverance wins reward.

Earnest thowt, an' constant striving,
Ever wi' one aim i'th' seet;
Tho' we may be late arrivin,
Yet at last we'st come in reight.

He who WILL succeed, he MUST,
When he's bid false hopes farewell.
If he firmly fix his trust
In his God, and in hissel,

Did yo Iver.

Gooid gracious! cried Susy, one fine summer's morn,
Here's a bonny to do! aw declare!
Aw wor niver soa capt sin th' day aw wor born!
Aw near saw sich a seet at a Fair.

Here, Sally! come luk! Ther's a maase made its nest
Reight ith' craan o' mi new Sundy bonnet!
Haiver its fun its way into this chist,
That caps me! Aw'm fast what to mak on it!

Its cut! Sithee thear! It's run reight under th' bed!
An luk here! What's'theas little things stirrin?
If they arn't some young uns at th' gooid-for-nowt's bred,
May aw be as deead as a herrin!

But what does ta say? "Aw mun draand 'em?" nooan soa!
Just luk ha they're seekin ther mother;
Shoo must be a poor little softheead to goa;
For awm nooan baan to cause her noa bother.

But its rayther to bad, just to mak her hooam thear,
For mi old en's net fit to be seen in
An' this new en, awm thinkin, ul luk rayther queer,
After sich a rum lot as thats been in.

But shut up awr pussy, an heed what aw say;
Yo mun keep a sharp e'e or shoo'll chait us;
Ah if shoo sees th' mother shoo'll kill it! An pray
What mun become o' thease poor helpless crayturs?

A'a dear! fowk have mich to be thankful for, yet,
'At's a roof o' ther own to cawer under,
For if we'd to seek ony nook we could get,
Whativer 'ud come on us aw wonder?

We should nooan on us like to be turned aat o' door,
Wi a lot a young bairns to tak 'care on:

Ah' although awm baat bonnet, an think misen poor,
What little aw have yo'st have t'share on.

That poor little maase aw dooant think meant me harm,
Shoo ne'er knew what that bonnet had cost me;
All shoo wanted wor some little nook snug an' warm,
An' a gooid two o'-three shillin its lost me.

Aw should think as they've come into th' world born i' silk,
They'll be aristocratical varmin;
But awm wasting mi time! awl goa get 'em some milk,
An' na daat but th' owd lass likes it warmin.

Bless mi life! a few drops 'll sarve them! If we try,
Awm weel sure we can easily spare 'em,
But as sooin as they're able, awl mak 'em all fly!
Never mind' if aw dooant! harum scarum!

An Old Man's Christmas Morning.

Its a long time sin' thee an' me have met befoor, owd lad, —
Soa pull up thi cheer, an' sit daan, for ther's noabdy moor welcome
nor thee:
Thi toppin's grown whiter nor once, — yet mi heart feels glad,
To see ther's a rooas o' thi cheek,an' a bit ov a leet i' thi e'e.

Thi limbs seem to totter an' shake, like a crazy owd fence,
'At th' wind maks to tremel an' creak; but tha still fills thi place;
An' it shows 'at tha'rt bless'd wi' a bit o' gradely gooid sense,
'At i' spite o' thi years an' thi cares, tha still wears a smile o' thi face.

Come fill up thi pipe — for aw knaw tha'rt reight fond ov a rick, —
An' tha'll find a drop o' hooarm-brew'd i' that pint up o'th' hob, aw
dar say;
An' nah, wol tha'rt toastin thi shins, just scale th' foir, an' aw'll side
thi owd stick,
Then aw'll tell thi some things 'ats happen'd sin tha went away.

An' first of all tha mun knaw 'at aw havn't been spar'd,

For trials an' troubles have come, an' mi heart has felt well nigh to
braik;
An' mi wife, 'at tha knaws wor mi pride, an' mi fortuns has shared,
Shoo bent under her griefs, an' shoo's flown far, far away aat o' ther
raik.

My life's like an owd gate 'ats nobbut one hinge for support,
An' sometimes aw wish—aw'm soa lonely— at tother 'ud drop off
wi' rust;
But it hasn't to be, for it seems Life maks me his spooart,
An' Deeath cannot even spare time, to turn sich an owd man into
dust.

Last neet as aw sat an' watched th' yule log awd put on to th' fire,
As it cracked, an' sparkled, an' flared up wi' sich gusto an' spirit,
An' when it wor touch'd it shone breeter, an' flared up still higher,
Till at last aw'd to shift th' cheer further back for aw couldn't bide
near it.

Th' dull saand o' th' church bells coom to tell me one moor Christmas mornin',
Had come, for its welcome—but ha could aw welcome it when all
aloan?
For th' snow wor fallin soa thickly, an' th' cold wind wor moanin,
An' them 'at aw lov'd wor asleep i' that cold church yard, under a
stoan:

Soa aw went to bed an' aw slept, an' then began dreamin,
'At mi wife stood by mi side, an' smiled, an' mi heart left off its beat-
in',
An' aw put aat mi hand, an' awoke, an' mornin' wor gleamin';
An' its made me feel sorrowful, an aw cannot give ovver freatin.

For aw think what a glorious Christmas day 'twod ha' been,
If awd goan to that place, where ther's noa moor cares,nor partin',
nor sorrow,
For aw know shoo's thear, or that dream aw sud nivver ha' seen,
But aw'll try to be patient, an' maybe shoo'll come fotch me to-
morrow.

It's forty' long summers an' winters, sin tha bade "gooid bye,"
An' as fine a young fella tha wor, as iver aw met i' mi life;
When tha went to some far away land, thi fortune to try,
An' aw stopt at hooam to toil on, becoss it wor th' wish o' my wife.

An' shoo wor a bonny young wench, an' better nor bonny,—
Aw seem nah as if aw can see her, wi' th' first little bairn on her
knee,
An' we called it Ann, for aw liked that name best ov ony,
An' fowk said it wor th' pictur o' th' mother, wi' just a strinklin o'
me.

An' th' next wor a lad, an' th' next wor a lad! then a lass came,—
That made us caant six,—an' six happier fowk niver sat to a meal,
An' they grew like hop plants—full o' life—but waikly i' th' frame,
An' at last one drooped, an' Deeath coom an' marked her with his
seal.

A year or two moor an' another seemed longin to goa,
An' all we could do wor to smooth his deeath bed, 'at he might
sleep sweeter—
Then th' third seemed to sicken an' pine, an' we couldn't say "noa,"
For he said his sister had called, an' he wor most anxious to meet
her—

An' how we watched th' youngest, noa mortal can tell but misen,
For we prized it moor, becoss it wor th' only one left us to cherish;
At last her call came, an' shoo luked sich a luk at us then,
Which aw ne'er shall forget, tho mi mem'ry ov all other things per-
ish.

A few years moor, when awr griefs wor beginnin to lighten,
Mi friends began askin my wife, if shoo felt hersen hearty an'
strong?
An' aw niver saw at her face wor beginning to whiten,
Till sho grew like a shadow, an' aw couldn't even guess wrong.

Then aw stood beside th' grave when th' saxton wor shovin in th'

gravel,
An' he said "this last maks five, an' aw think ther's just room for another,"
An' aw went an' left him, lonely an' heartsick to travel,
Till th' time comes when aw may lig daan beside them four bairns an' ther mother.

An' aw think what a glorious Christmas day 'twod ha been
If aw'd gooan to that place where ther's noa moor cares, nor partin, nor sorrow;
An aw knaw they're thear, or that dream aw should niver ha seen,
But aw'll try to be patient, an' maybe shoo'll come fotch me to-morrow.

Billy Bumble's Bargain.

Young Billy Bumble bowt a pig,
Soa aw've heeard th' neighbors say;
An' mony a mile he had to trig
One sweltin' summer day;
But Billy didn't care a fig,
He said he'd mak it pay;
He *knew* it wor a bargain,
An' he cared net who said nay.

He browt it hooam to Ploo Croft loin,
But what wor his surprise
To find all th' neighbors standing aat,
We oppen maaths an' eyes;
"By gow!" sed Billy, to hissen,
"This pig *must* be a prize!"
An' th' wimmen cried, "Gooid gracious fowk!
But isn't it a size?"

Then th' chaps sed, "Billy, where's ta been?
Whativer has ta browt?
That surely isn't crayture, lad,
Aw heeard 'em say tha'd bowt?
It luks moor like a donkey,

Does ta think 'at it con rawt?"
But Billy crack'd his carter's whip.
An' answered' em wi' nowt.

An' reight enuff it war a pig,
If all they say is true,
Its length war five foot eight or nine,
Its height wor four foot two;
An' when it coom to th' pig hoil door,
He couldn't get it through,
Unless it went daan ov its knees,
An' that it wodn't do.

Then Billy's mother coomed to help,
An' hit it wi' a mop;
But thear it wor, an' thear it seem'd
Detarmined it 'ud stop;
But all at once it gave a grunt,
An' oppen'd sich a shop;
An' finding aat 'at it wor lick'd,
It laup'd clean ovver th' top.

His mother then shoo shook her heead,
An' pool'd a woeful face;
"William," shoo sed, "tha shouldn't bring
Sich things as theas to th' place.
Aw hooap tha art'nt gooin to sink
Thi mother i' disgrace;
But if tha buys sich things as thease
Aw'm feared it will be th' case!"

"Nah, mother, niver freat." sed Bill,
"Its one aw'm goin to feed,
Its rayther long i'th' legs, aw know,
But that's becoss o'th' breed;
If its a trifle long i'th' grooin,
Why hang it! niver heed!
Aw know its net a beauty,
But its cheap, it is, indeed!"

"Well time 'ul try," his mother sed, —
An' time at last did try;
For niver sich a hungry beeast
Had been fed in a sty.
"What's th' weight o'th' long legged pig, Billy!"
Wor th' neighbors' daily cry;
"Aw connot tell yo yet," sed Bill,
"Aw'll weigh it bye an' bye."

An' hard poor Billy persevered,
But all to noa avail,
It swallow'd all th' mait it could get,
An' wod ha' swallow'd th' pail;
But Billy took gooid care to stand
O'th' tother side o'th' rail;
But fat it didn't gain as mich
As what 'ud greeas its tail.

Pack after pack o' mail he bowt,
Until he'd bought fourteen;
But net a bit o' difference
I'th' pig wor to be seen:
Its legs an' snowt wor just as long
As iver they had been;
Poor Billy caanted rib bi rib
An' heaved a sigh between.

One day he, mix'd a double feed,
An' put it into th' troff;
"Tha greedy lukkin beeast," he sed,
"Aw'll awther stawl thee off,
Or else aw'll brust thi hide — that is
Unless 'at its to toff!"
An' then he left it wol he went
His mucky clooas to doff.

It worn't long befoor he coom
To see ha matters stood;

He luk'd at th' troff, an' thear it wor,
Five simple bits o' wood,
As cleean scraped aat as if it had
Ne'er held a bit o' food;
"Tha slotch!" sed Bill, "aw do believe
Tha'd ait me if tha could."

Next day he browt a butcher,
For his patience had been tried,
An' wi a varry deeal to do,
Its legs wi rooap they tied;
An' then his shinin knife he drew
An' stuck it in its side —
It mud ha been a crockadile,
Bi th' thickness ov its hide.

But blooid began to flow, an' then
Its long legg'd race wor run;
They scalded, scraped, an' hung it up,
An' when it all wor done,
Fowk coom to guess what weight it wor,
And mony a bit o' fun
They had, for Billy's mother said
"It ought to weigh a ton."

Billy wor walkin up an' daan,
Dooin nowt but fume an' fidge!
He luk'd at th' pig — then daan he set,
I'th nook o'th' window ledge,
He saw th' back booan wor sticken aght,
Like th' thin end ov a wedge;
It luk'd like an' owd blanket
Hung ovver th' winterhedge.

His mother rooar'd an' th' wimmen sigh'd,
But th' chaps did nowt but laff;
Poor Billy he could hardly bide,
To sit an' hear ther chaff —
Then up he jumped, an' off he run,

But whear fowk niver knew;
An' what wor th' warst, when mornin' coom,
Th' deead pig had mizzled too.

Th' chaps wander'd th' country far an' near,
Until they stall'd thersen;
But nawther Billy nor his pig
Coom hooam agean sin then;
But oft fowk say, i'th' deead o'th' neet,
Near Shibden's ruined mill,
The gooast o' Billy an' his pig
May be seen runnin still.

Moral.

Yo fowk 'ats tempted to goa buy
Be careful what yo do;
Dooant be persuaded coss "its *cheap*,"
For if yo do yo'll rue;
Dooant think its lowerin to yor sen
To ax a friend's advice,
Else like poor Billy's pig, 't may be
Bowt dear at ony price.

Rejected.

Gooid bye, lass, aw dunnot blame,
Tho' mi loss is hard to bide!
For it wod ha' been a shame,
Had tha ivver been the bride
Of a workin chap like me;
One 'ats nowt but love to gie.

Hard hoot'd neives like thease o' mine.
Surely ne'er wor made to press
Hands so lily-white as thine;
Nor should arms like thease caress
One so slender, fair, an' pure,
'Twor unlikely, lass, aw'm sure.

But thease tears aw cannot stay,
Drops o' sorrow fallin fast,
Hopes once held aw've put away
As a dream, an think its past;
But mi poor heart loves thi still,
An' wol life is mine it will.

When aw'm seated, lone and sad,
Wi mi scanty, hard won meal,
One thowt still shall mak me glad,
Thankful that alone aw feel
What it is to tew an'strive
Just to keep a soul alive.

Th' whin-bush rears o'th' moor its form,
An' wild winds rush madly raand,
But it whistles to the storm,
In the barren home it's faand;
Natur fits it to be poor,
An 'twor vain to strive for moor.

If it for a lily sighed,
An' a lily chonced to grow,
When it found the fair one died,
Powerless to brave the blow
Of the first rude gust o' wind,
Which had left its wreck behind.

Then 'twod own 'twor better fate
Niver to ha' held the prize;
Whins an' lilies connot mate,
Sich is not ther destinies;
Then 'twor wrang for one like me,
One soa poor, to sigh for thee.

Then gooid bye, aw dunnot blame,
Tho' mi loss it's hard to bide,
For it wod ha' been a shame

Had tha iver been mi bride;
Content aw'll wear mi lonely lot,
Tho' mi poor heart forgets thee not.

Duffin Johnie.

(A Rifleman's Adventure.)

Th' mooin shone breet wi silver leet,
An' th' wind wor softly sighin,
Th' burds did sleep, an' th' snails did creep,
An' th' buzzards wor a flying;
Th' daisies donned ther neet caps on,
An' th buttercups wor weary,
When Jenny went to meet her John,
Her Rifleman, her dearie.

Her Johnny seemed as brave a lad
As iver held a rifle,
An' if ther wor owt in him bad,
'Twor nobbut just a trifle
He wore a suit o' sooity grey,
To show 'at he wor willin
To feight for th' Queen and country
When perfect in his drillin.

His heead wor raand, his back wor straight,
His legs wor long an' steady,
His fist wor fully two pund weight,
His heart wor true an' ready;
His upper lip wor graced at th' top
Wi mustache strong and bristlin,
It railly wor a spicy crop;
Yo'd think to catch him whistlin.

His buzzum burned wi' thowt's o' war,
He long'd for battles clatter.

He grieved to think noa foeman dar
To cross a sup o' watter;
He owned one spot,—an' nobbut one,
Within his heart wor tender,
An' as his darlin had it fun,
He'd be her bold defender.

At neet he donn'd his uniform,
War trials to endure,
An' helped his comrades brave, to storm
A heap ov horse manure!
They said it wor a citidel,
Fill'd wi' some hostile power,
They boldly made a breach, and well
They triumph'd in an hour.

They did'nt wade to th' knees i' blooid,
(That spoils one's breeches sadly),
But th' pond o' sypins did as gooid,
An' scented 'em as badly;
Ther wor noa slain to hug away,
Noa heeads, noa arms wor wantin,
They lived to feight another day,
An' spend ther neets i' rantin.

Brave Johnny's rooad wor up a loin
Where all wor dark an' shaded,
Part grass, part stooans, part sludge an' slime
But quickly on he waded;
An' nah an' then he cast his e'e
An luk'd behund his shoulder.
He worn't timid, noa net he!
He crack'd, "he knew few bolder."

But once he jumped, an' said "Oh dear!"
Becoss a beetle past him,
But still he wor unknown to fear,
He'd tell yo if yo asked him;
He couldn't help for whispering once,

This loin's a varry long un,
A chap wod have but little chonce
Wi thieves, if here amang em.

An' all at once he heeard a voice
Cry out, "Stand and deliver!
Your money or your life, mak choice,
Before your brains I shiver;"
He luk'd all raand, but failed to see
A sign of livin craytur,
Then tremlin dropt upon his knee,
Fear stamp'd on ivery faytur.

"Gooid chap," he said, "mi rifle tak,
Mi belts, mi ammunition,
Aw've nowt but th' clooas at's o' mi back
Oh pity mi condition;
Aw wish aw'd had a lot o' brass,
Aw'd gie thi ivery fardin;
Aw'm nobbut goin to meet a lass,
At Tate's berry garden."

"Aw wish shoo wor, aw daoant care where,
Its her fault aw've to suffer;"
Just then a whisper in his ear
Said, "Johnny, thar't a duffer,"
He luk'd, an' thear claise to him stuck
Wor Jenny, burst wi' lafter;
"A'a, John," shoo says, "Aw've tried thi pluck,
Aw'st think o' this at after."

"An when tha tells what thinga tha'll do,
An' booasts o' manly courage,
Aw'st tell thi then, as nah aw do,
Go hooam an' get thi porrige."
"Why Jenny wor it thee," he said
"Aw fancied aw could spy thi,
Aw nobbut reckoned to be flaid,
Aw did it but to trie thi."

"Just soa," shoo says, "but certain 'tis
Aw hear thi heart a beatin,
An' tak this claat to wipe thi phiz
Gooid gracious, ha tha'rt sweeatin;
Thar't brave noa daat, an' tha can crow
Like booastin cock-a-doodle,
But nooan sich men for me, aw vow,
When wed, aw'll wed a 'noodle.'

Lost Love.

Shoo wor a bonny, bonny lass
Her een as black as sloas,
Her hair a flying' thunner claad,
Her cheeks a blowing rooas;
Her smile coom like a sunny gleam
Her cherry lips to curl;
Her voice wor like a murm'ring stream
At flowed through banks o' pearl.

Aw long'd to claim her for mi own,
But nah mi love is crost;
An aw mun wander on alooan,
An' mourn for her aw've lost.

Aw couldn't ax her to be mine,
Wi' poverty at th' door:
Aw niver thowt breet een could shine
Wi' love for one so poor;
But nah ther's summat i' mi breast,
Tells me aw miss'd mi way:
An' lost that lass I loved th' best
Throo fear shoo'd say me nay.

Aw long'd to claim her for, &c.,

Aw saunter'd raand her cot at morn,
An' oft i'th' dark o'th' neet;

Aw've knelt mi daan i'th loin to find
Prints ov her tiny feet:
An' under th' window, like a thief,
Aw've crept to hear her spaik,
An' then aw've hurried home agean
For fear mi heart ud braik.

Aw long'd to claim her for, &c.,

Another bolder nor misen,
Has robb'd me o' mi dear,
An' nah aw ne'er may share her joy
An' ne'er may dry her tear;
But though aw'm heartsick, lone, an' sad,
An' though hope's star is set,
To know she's lov'd as aw'd ha' lov'd
Wod mak me happy yet.

Aw long'd to claim her for, &c.,

Th' Traitle Sop.

Once in a little country taan
A grocer kept a shop,
And sell'd amang his other things,
Prime traitle drink and pop,

Teah, coffee, currans, spenish juice,
Soft soap an' paader blue,
Presarves an' pickles, cinnamon,
Allspice an' pepper too;

An' hoasts o' other sooarts o' stuff
To sell to sich as came,
As figs, an' raisens, salt an' spice,
Too numerous to name.

One summer's day a waggon stood
Just opposite his door,

An' th' childer all gaped raand as if
They'd ne'er seen one afoor;

An' in it wor a traitle cask,
It wor a wopper too,
To get it aat they all wor fast
Which iver way to do;

But wol they stood an parley'd thear,
Th' horse gave a sudden chuck,
An' aat it flew, an' bursting threw
All th' traitle into th' muck.

Then th' childer laff'd an' clapp'd their hands,
To them it seem'd rare fun,
But th' grocer ommost lost his wits
When he saw th' traitle run;

He stamp'd an' raved, an' then declared
He wodn't pay a meg,
An'th' carter vow'd until he did
He wodn't stir a peg.

He said he'd done his business reight,
He'd brought it up to th' door,
An thear it wor, an' noa fair chap
Wad want him to do moor.

But wol they stamped, an' raved, an' swore,
An' vented aat ther spleen,
Th' childer wor thrang enough, you're sure,
All plaisterd up to th' een,

A neighbor chap saw th' state o' things,
An' pitied ther distress,
An' begg'd em not to be soa sour
Abaat soa sweet a mess;

"An' tha'd be sour," th'owd grocer said,

If th' job wor thine, owd lad,
An' somdy wanted thee to pay
For what tha'd niver had.

"Th' fault isn't mine," said th' cart driver
"My duty's done I hope?
I've brought him traitle, thear it is,
An' he mun sam it up."

Soa th' neighbor left em to thersen,
He'd nowt noa moor to say,
But went to guard what ther wor left,
And send th' young brood away:

This didn't suit th' young lads a bit,
They didn't mean to stop,
They felt detarmin'd 'at they'd get
Another traitle sop.

They tried all ways, but th' chap stood firm,
They couldn't get a lick,
An' some o' th' boldest gate a taste
O'th neighbor's walkin sticks

At last one said, I know a plan
If we can scheam to do it,
We'll knock one daan bang into th' dolt,
An' let him roll reight throo it;

Agreed, agreed! they all replied,
An here comes little Jack,
He's foorced to pass cloise up this side,
We'll do it in a crack.

Poor Jack war rather short, an' coom
Just like a suckin duck,
He little dream'd at th' sweets o' life
Wod iver be his luck;

But daan they shoved him, an' he roll'd
Heead first bang into th' mess,
An' aat he coom a woeful sight,
As yo may easy guess.

They marched him off i' famous glee
All stickified an' clammy,
Then licked him clean an' sent him hooam
To get lick'd by his mammy.

Then th' cartdriver an th' grocer coom
Boath in a dreadful flutter,
To save some, but they coom too lat,
It all wor lost ith gutter:

It towt a lesson to 'em boath
Before that job wor ended,
To try (at stead o' falling aat)
If ought went wrang to mend it.

For wol fowk rave abaat ther loss,
Some sharper's sure to pop,
An' aat o' ther misfortunes
They'll contrive to get a sop. —

To Let.

Aw live in a snug little cot,
An' tho' poor, yet aw keep aat o' debt,
Cloise by, in a big garden plot,
Stands a mansion, 'at long wor to let.

Twelve month sin' or somewhear abaat,
A fine lukin' chap donned i' black,
Coom an' luk'd at it inside an' aat
An' decided this mansion to tak.

Ther wor whiteweshers coom in a drove
An' masons, an' joiners, an' sweeps,

An' a blacksmith to fit up a cove,
An' bricks, stooans an' mortar i' heaps.

Ther wor painters, an' glazzeners too,
To mend up each bit ov a braik,
An' a lot 'at had nowt else to do,
But to help some o'th 'tothers to laik.

Ther wor fires i' ivery range,
They niver let th' harston get cooiled,
Throo th' celler to th' thack they'd a change,
An' iverything all in a mooild.

Th' same chap 'at is th' owner o'th' Hall,
Is th' owner o'th' cot whear aw dwell,
But if aw ax for th' leeast thing at all;
He tells me to do it mysel.

This hall lets for fifty a year,
Wol five paand is all 'at aw pay;
When th' day come mi rent's allus thear,
An' that's a gooid thing in its way,

At th' last all th' repairers had done,
An' th' hall wor as cleean as a pin,
Aw wor pleased when th' last lot wor gooan,
For aw'd getten reight sick o' ther din.

Then th' furniture started to come,
Waggon looads on it, all spankin new,
Rich crimson an' gold covered some,
Wol some shone i' scarlet an' blue.

Ov sofas aw think hauf a scoor,
An' picturs enuff for a show?
They fill'd ivery corner awm sure,
Throo th' garret to th' kitchen below.

One day when a cab drove to th' gate,
Th' new tenant stept aat, an' his wife,
An' tawk abaat fashion an state!
Yo ne'er saw sich a spread i' yor life.

Ther war sarvents to curtsey 'em in,
An' aw could'nt help sayin', "bi'th mass;"
As th' door shut when they'd booath getten in,
"A'a its grand to ha' plenty o' brass."

Ther wor butchers, an' bakers, an' snobs,
An' grocers, an' milkmen, an' snips,
All seekin' for orders an' jobs,
An' sweetenin th' sarvents wi' tips.

Aw sed to th' milk-chap tother day,
"Ha long does ta trust sich fowk, Ike?
Each wick aw'm expected to pay,"
"Fine fowk," he says, "pay when they like."

Things went on like this, day bi day,
For somewhear cloise on for a year,
Wol aw ne'er thowt o' lukkin' that way;
Altho' aw wor livin soa near.

But one neet when awd finished mi wark,
An' wor tooastin mi shins anent th' fire,
A chap rushes in aat 'o'th' dark
Throo heead to fooit plaistered wi' mire.

Says he, "does ta know whear they've gooan?"
Says aw, "Lad, pray, who does ta meean?"
"Them 'at th' hall," he replied, wi a grooan,
"They've bolted an' diddled us cleean."

Aw tell'd him 'aw'd ne'er heeard a word,
He cursed as he put on his hat,
An' he sed, "well, they've flown like a burd,
An' paid nubdy owt, an' that's what."

He left, an' aw crept off to bed,
Next day awd a visit throo Ike,
But aw shut up his maath when aw sed,
"Fine fowk tha knows pay when they like."

Ther's papers ith' winders, "to let,"
An' aw know varry weel ha 't 'll be;

They'll do th' same for th' next tenant awl bet,
Tho they neer' do a hawpoth for me.

But aw let 'em do just as they pleease,
Awm content tho' mi station is low,
An' awm thankful sich hard times as thease
If aw manage to pay what aw owe.

This precept, friends, niver forget,
For a wiser one has not been sed,
Be detamined to rise aat o' debt
Tho' yo go withaat supper to bed,—'

Fault Finders.

If ther's ony sooart o' fowk aw hate, it's them at's allus lukkin'
aght for faults;—hang it up! they get soa used to it, wol they willn't
see ony beauties if they are thear. They remind me ov a chap 'at aw
knew at wed a woman 'at had a wart at th' end ov her nooas, but it
war nobbut a little en, an' shoo wor a varry bonny lass for all that;
but when they'd been wed a bit, an' th' newness had getten warn
off, he began to fancy at this wart grew bigger ivery day, an' he
stared at it, an' studied abaght it, wol when he luk'd at his wife he
could see nowt else, an' he kept dinging her up wi' it wol shoo felt
varry mich troubled. But one day, as they wor gettin' ther dinner, he
said, "Nay, lass, aw niver did see sich a thing as that wart o' thy
nooas is growing into; if it gooas on tha'll be like a rhynockoroo or a
newnicorn or summat!"

"Well," shoo says, "when tha wed me tha wed th' wart an' all, an'
if tha doesn't like it tha con lump it."

"Aw've noa need to lump it," he says, "for it's lumpin' itsen or
aw'll gie nowt for it."

Soa they went on, throo little to moor, till they'd a regular fratch,
an' as sooin as' he'd getten his dinner, he off to his wark, an' shoo to
her mother's. When Jim coom back an' fan th' fire aght, an' noa wife,
he felt rayther strange, but he wor detarmined to let her see 'at he
could do baat her, soa he gate a bit o' summat to ait an' went to bed.
This went on for two-o'-three days, an' he wor as miserable as iver
he could be, but o'th' Setterdy he happened to meet her i'th' sham-

bles, an' they booath stopped an' grinned, for they'd nowt agean one another i'th' bothem.

"Nah, lass," he said, "aw think it's abaat time for thee to come hooam."

"Nay, aw'll come nooan," shoo says, "till aw've getten shut o' this wart."

"Oh, ne'er heed that, lass; it doesn't luk hauf as big as it did, an' if tha wor all wart, aw'd rayther have thi nor be as aw am."

"Soa shoo went back wi' him, an' throo that time to this he's allus luk'd for her beauties asteead ov her faults, an they get on swimmingly. One day shoo axed him if he thowt th' wart wor ony bigger?" "A'a lass," he sed, "thi een are soa breet, aw didn't know tha had one!"

— — — — — — — — —

What aw want yo to do is to be charitable, an' if yo find ony faults, think—yo happen may have one or two yorsen. Ther's net monny on us 'at's killed wi sense, but he hasn't th' leeast at's enuff to know he's a fooil.

This world wad be a better spot,
Wi' joys moor thickly strown,
If fowk cared less for others' faults
An tried to mend ther own.

There's plenty o' room for us all to mend, an' them 'at set abaat it sooinest are likely to be perfect furst; at ony rate, if we try it'll show willin'.

Disapointment.

"Blessed are they who expect nothing, for they shall net be disappointed."

Aw once knew a chap they called old Sammy; he used ta gaa wi a donkey, an th' mooast remarkable things abaat him wor his clogs an' his rags. Sammy had niver been wed, tho' he war fifty years old, but it wor allus believed he'd managed ta save a bit a' brass. One day he war gain up Hepenstull Bunk, Jenny o' Jooans a' th' Long Lover wor goin up befoor him, an' whether it wor at her clogs were made a' his favrite pattern, or her ancles had summat abaat 'em different to what he'd iver seen befoor, aw cannot tell, but it seems a feelin coom ovver him all at once, sich as he'd niver had befoor, an' when he'd managed ta overtak her, he sed, "It's loaning for heeat aw think, Jenny." "Eea, aw think its likely for bein wut," shoo sed. "Awve just been thinkin," sed Sammy, "at if I wornt na a single old chap, aw shouldn't have to trail up an' daan in a lot a' rags like thease, for awm sure this jacket has hardly strength to hing o' mi rig, an' mi britches are soa full o' hoils wol awm feeared sometimes when awm puttin em on, at awst tummel throo an braik my neck." "Well, reight enuff, a woife's varry useful at times," shoo sed, "but as tha hasn't one if tha'll learn mi thi jacket, aw'll see if it cannot be mended far thi a bit." "Aw allus thowt tha war a gooid sooart, Jenny, an' awl tak thi at thi word," he sed: so he pool'd off his coit an gave it her an' it were arranged 'at he should call for it next neet. You may bet yor life he didn't forget, an when he saw it mended up, an' brushed wol it luk'd ommost as gooid as new, he luk'd first at it an then at her, an at last he sed, "Aw think we should be able to get on varry weel together, what says ta?" Aw dooant know what shoo sed, but it wornt long befoor they wor wed, for Sammy thowt shoo'd be worth her mait if it wor nobbut for mendin up his old duds. They hadn't been wed long, when he axed her to mend his britches. — "A'a," shoo sed, "Aw cannot mend em, aw niver could sew i' mi life!" "Why that is a tale," he sed, "tha mended mi jacket all reight!" "Nay, indeed aw nawther! — Aw mended nooon on it! Aw sent it to th' tailor an paid for it doin." "Then awm dropt on," sed Sammy, "for aw expected tha'd be able to do all sich like wark." "Tha should niver expect owt an' then tha willnt get dropt on," shoo sed. — "That, wor a bit o' varry gooid advice.

Work Away.

BONNY lads, and bonny lasses!
Work away! work away!
Think how swift each moment passes,
Time does never stay.

Then let's up and to our labours,
They who *will*, must sure succeed,
He does best who best endeavours, —
Try again shall be our creed.

New Machinery &c.

It shows varry little sense for fowk to object to a new machine till they've tried it, or to fancy it'll be th' means o' smashin th' trade. Luk at th' paaer looms; when they I wor started all th' hand-loom weyvers struck wark, becoss they said it ud do 'em all up, an' ther'd be noa wark at all for weyvers in a bit; but it hasn't turn'd aat soa, for ther's moor weyvers i'th' country to-day, nor iver ther wor; and they addle moor brass, an' awm sure they've easier wark. For if this country doesn't get new machines, other countries will, an' when we're left behund hand an' connot meet 'em i'th' market, we'st be a deeal war off nor ony new invention can mak us. All at's been done soa far has helped to mak us better off. They connot mak a machine to think, they're forced to stop thear; an' aw dooant daat if we'd to live long enuff, ther'd be a time when chaps ud ha nowt to do but think-but it's to be hoaped 'at they'd have summat else to think abaat nor rattenin', or shooitin', or ruinin' fowk. Aw've tawk'd to some abaat it, an' they say they're foorced to do sum way to keep wages up, but if aw can tell em ha to mak brass goa farther, they'll be content to give up th' Union. But aw think it goas far enuff — what they want is to keep it nearer hooam, to let less on it goa to th' ale haase, to spend less o' dog feightin', pigeon flyin', an' rat worryin'; an' if they'd niver spend owt withaat think in' whether it wor for ther gooid or net, they'd find a deal moor brass i'th' drawer corner at th' month end, an' varry likely a nice little bit to fall back on i'th' Savings bank at th' year end. An a chap stands hauf an inch heigher when he's a bankbook in his pocket; an' butchers and grocers varry sooin begin to nod at him, an' ax if they can do owt for him. But if he goas on th'strap, an' happens to be a month behund, he's foorced to stand o' one side till iverybody else gets sarved, an' then if he doesn't like what's left they tell him to goa leave it. It isn't what a chap addles, it's what a chap saves 'at makes him rich.

Sellin' drink has made mony a chap rich, an suppin it has made thaasands poor. But still aw must honestly say 'at aw cannot agree wi' teetotalism altogether. If noa men gate drunken, ther'd be noa need for anybody to sign th' pledge;—an' aw dooant think they goa th' reight way to get fowk to be sober. They publish papers, but what use is made on em? Yo hardly iver see a midden emptied but what yo'll find two or three pieces o'th' "British Workman," or th' "Temperance Advocate" flyin' abaat; an' they hold meetings an' spend a sight o' brass o' printin' an' praichin', an' still they doant mak one teetotaller 'at ov a thaasand. Aw should advise em to try this way. Let em offer a #500 prize for him 'at can invent a drink as gooid takin' as ale—an' one, 'at willn't mak fowk drunk. Chaps mun sup summat when they're away throo hooam, an it is'nt iverybody's stumach 'at's strong enuff to tak watter, unless it's let daan wi sum-mat; an' ther is noa teetotal drink invented yet 'at's any better nor Spenish- juice-watter. They're all like pap. Coffee an' tea are all weel enuff, but if yo want that yo munnot goa to a Temperance Hotel for it. Aw'ye tried it monny a scoor times, but aw niver gate owt fit to sup, an' if it hadn't been for th' drop o' rum aw gate 'em to put into it, aw couldn't ha swallowed it. Tea an' coffee are things 'at dooant mend wi' warmin up, an' yo connot allus wait woll fowk mak it, an' soa if yo want to sup yo mun awther goa an' beg a drop o' watter, or pay fourpence for a glass o' belly vengeance, or yo mun get a glass o' drink—but yo've noa need to get a dozzen. Teetotallers say it contains poison, an' noa daat it does—but it's of a varry slow mak, an' if yo niver goa to excess yo may live to be a varry owd man, an' dee befoor it begins to operate, Ther wor once a chap killed hissel wi' aitin traitle parkin, but that's noa reason we shouldn't have a bit o' brandy-snap at our fair. Aw allus think a teetotal lecturer is like a bottle o' pop. Ther's a bit ov a crack to 'start wi', an' a gooid deal o' fooamin, an' frothin', an' fizzin', but when it's all ovver, an' settled daan, what's left is varry poor stuff. Still aw think one teetotaller is worth moor nor a ship-load o' drunkards.

September Month.

Blackberries are ripe in September, an' we may consider th' year's ripe, for when this month gets turned, things 'll begin o' gooin' th' back way. Its vany wonderful when we look reight at it. This world's a wonderful spot, an' ther's a deal o' wonderful things in it. Ther's some things at it's varry wonderful to see, an' ther's some things' at it's wonderful net to see. Aw thowt it wor varry wonderful, a week or two sin', when aw pass'd Stanninley Station, 'at ther worn't a chap wi' a dog under his arm; it's th' furst time aw iver pass'd an' didn't see one. But aw niver think it's wonderful for ther to be a fooil in a company; an' aw dooant think its wonderful when aw find 'at th' biggest fooil has allus th' mooast to say.

Nah, its a varry nice time o'th' year is this for fowk to have a bit of a pic-nic;—aw dooant know owt 'at's a better excuse for a chap to tighten his belly-band nor a pic-nic, becoss iverybody taks twice as mich stuff to ait as they know they'll want, for fear fowk might think they wor shabby. If yo get a invite to a doo o' that mak', be sure yo goa, if you've owt of a twist. But talkin' abaat invites maks me study a bit. When yo get an invitation, allus think it ovver befoor yo tak' it Ax yorsen one or two questions abaat it. If yo think it's becoss yo can play th' peanner, or becoss yo can sing—tell 'em yorterms. If yo think it's becoss some owd uncle is likely to dee an' leeav yo a lot o' brass, an' they've a dowter or two 'at isn't wed— tell 'em yor engaged (to a lady). If yo think it's becoss they fancy yor a shinin' leet—tell 'em yo're gooan aat. I yo think it's becoss they want to borrow some brass, an' yor daatful whether yo'll iver get it back agean—tell 'em yo've soa monny calls made on yo, wall yo're feeard yo connot call o' them at present. But if yo think it's just becoss they want yo, an' they'll be glad to see yo,' put on yor hat an' off in a minit.

Aw once knew a chap 'at had getten a invite to a doo, an' he wor gooin' to tak his wife wi' him; an' he wor tellin' some mates what a shimmer shoo wor gooin' to cut. "Mun," he says, "sho'll just luk like one o' them figures i'th' waxworks! Aw've bowt her a goold cheen as thick as my thum; it's cost ornmost a paand. An' tawk abaat a dress! why, yo' niver saw sich a dress it's a real Mary Antique! Th' chap 'at sell'd it me, said it had been made for th' Princess o' Wales, but it wor soa mich brass wol th' Prince couldn't affoord to pay for't, so he let me have it cheap; an' it's just like buckram—it'll stand ov an end." "Why," said one o'th' chaps, "the Princess willn't be suited if shoo hears tell 'at thy wife's gettin' it." "Noa," he said, "aw dooant think shoo wod, but awst noan tell her; an' if shoo gets to know, she mun try an' put up wi' a bit ov a trial nah an' then. Ther's allus troubles for th' rich as weel as th' poor." Well! all this gooas to prove what aw said at th' startin'—it's a wonderful world, an' ther's a deeal o' wonderful things in it;—an', to quote from the poet (Milton aw think), aw may say—

It's a varry' gooid world that we live in
To lend, or to spend, or to give in;—
But to beg, or to borrow, or get a man's own,
It's th' varry worst world 'at iver wor known.

Hi, an' its th' best 'at iver wor known yet; an haiver mich fowk may say agean it, awve allus nooatised at' ther's varry few seem inclined to part wi' it.

A Hawporth.

Whear is thi' Daddy doy? Whear is thi' mam?
What are ta cryin for, poor little lamb?
Dry up thi peepies, pet, wipe thi wet face;
Tears o' thy little cheeks seem aat 'o place.
What do they call thi, lad? Tell me thi name;
Have they been ooinion thi? Why, its a shame.
Here, tak this hawpny, an' buy thi some spice,
Rocksticks or humbugs or summat 'at's nice.
Then run of hooam agean, fast as tha can;
Thear,—thart all reight agean; run like a man.

He wiped up his tears wi his little white brat,
An' he tried to say summat, aw couldn't tell what;
But his little face breeten'd wi' pleasure all throo:—
A'a!—its cappin, sometimes, what a hawpny can do.

Buttermilk &c.

May is the month for Buttermilk! A doctor once tell'd me it wor worth a guinea a pint; he sed it licked cod liver oil, castor oil; or paraffin oil. Castor oil, he said, war varry gooid for ther bowels, cod liver oil for ther liver, an' paraffin oil for ther leets (whear they'd noa gas), but buttermilk wor better nor all three put together, an' he ad vised me to tak it. "Why," aw sed; "what's th' use o'. me takkin it when aw dooant ail owt?" "Ther's noa tellin' ha sooin yo may," he said, "an' an it's a varry simple remedy, yo'd better tak it whether yo do or net." "Reight enuff," aw sed, "simple things sometimes do th' best. Aw once knew a woman 'at had been confined to her bed for twelve year, an' her husband cured her in a minit, after all th' doctors at th' infirmary had gien her up." Th' doctor pricked his ears when aw sed soa, an' wanted to know all abaat it, soa aw at it an' tell'd him. "Sally an' her husband lived at th' Arred Well, but he oft used to goa as far as th' Coit Hill ova neet to have a pint an' enjoy an haar or two i' company, an' when he gate haoam he used to catch it, an' finely too, aw con assure yo, for altho shood ligg'd i' bed soa long, shoo had'nt lost th' use ov her tongue, an' her felly said 'at shoo hadn't lost th' use ov her teeth nawther, for shoo could ait as weel as iver shoo could. One neet as he wor gooin hooam, he bethowt him he'd try a bit ov a dodge on, for although he felt varry sooary for his wife, yet he could'nt help thinkin' it wor partly consait at shoo'd suffer'd throo; soa when he gate in, shoo began a blowin' into him i' fine style. 'Th' owd time, lad! It shows what tha cares for me! Aw hav'nt had a wick soul to spaik to sin tha went aat, but it's all one to thee! Tha'll come hooam some time an' find me ligg'd deead, an' then tha can spree abaat throo morm to neet.' 'Nay, lass, aw dooant think aw should spree abaat any moor nor aw do nah. But who does ta think aw met to neet?' he said. 'Ah know nowt abaat it, nor care nawther.' 'Why, but as aw war comin' up bith' Brayvet Gate, aw met Betty Earnshaw, an' soa aw went gaiterds wi her a bit, an' that's reason aw'm soa lat.' 'Oh! tha mud weel be lat! Shoo war an' owd sweetheart o' thine, wor Betty.' 'Eea, shoo war axin me ha tha wor gettin' on, shoo seems vany sooary for thi.' 'Sooary be hanged! aw want nooan ov her sooarys! If shoo could nobbut get me aat o' th' gate, shoo'd be all reight. Did shoo ax when tha thowt tha'd be at liberty?' 'Nay shoo did'nt, but shoo did say at shoo thowt tha lasted long, but shoo pitied thee an' me.' 'Pitied thee, did shoo! An' what did shoo pity thi for, aw should like to know? Shoo happen thowt shoo could do better for thee nor what aw've done, but if shoo wor as badly as me shood know summat. 'Eea, but shoo isn't, for aw nivver saw her luk better i' mi life, an' shoo talks abaat commin' i'th' morn in' to clean up for thi a bit; aw sed tha'd be fain to see her, an' tha sees if owt should happen thee, shadd be getten into th' way a bit, an' begin to feel moor used to th' haase.' 'Niver! wol my heart's warm, Tom. Aw'll niver have sich a huzzy i'th' haase, wheal' aw am! aw'm nooan done wi yet! aw'll live a bit longer to plague yo wi', an' as for cleanin', aw'll crawl abaat o' mi hands an' knees afoor shoo shall do owt for me! Yo think aw'm poorly an' soa aw'm to be trodden on, but aw'll let yo see awm worth a dozen deead uns yet; nasty owd ponse as shoo is!" An' as sure as yor thear, Doctor, shoo gate up th' next morn in' an' kinneld th' fair, an' when Tom coom hoam to his braikfast all wor ready, an' shoo wor set daan at th' table wi a clean cap on, an' lukkin as smart as smart could be. When th' chap saw this, he said, "Lass, aw think aw'd better send Betty backward," "Eea, aw think tha had," shoo sed, "an' th'a can send her word throo me 'at aw may live to donee on her gravestooan yet." Tom bafs in his sleeve a bit sometimes, an' if iver one ov her owd fits seems likely ta come on, he's nowt to do but say a word or two abaat Betty, an' shoo's reight in a minnit. That licks buttermilk, Doctor.

It's a comfort.

It's a comfort a chap can do withaat what he connot get. It feels hard to have to do wi' less nor what a body has at present, but if it has to be it will be, an' it's cappin' ha' fowk manage to pool throo haiver bad th' job is. It's naa use for a chap to keep longin' for sum mat better, unless he's willin' to buckle to, an' work for it; an' a chap wi' an independent mind ne'er freeats becoss he hasn't all he wants; he sets hissen to get it, an' if he's detarmined he oft succeeds, an' if net he doesn't sit daan an' mump, but up an' at it agean. Havin' a lot o' brass doesn't mak a chap happy, but spend in' it may do, an' if a chap's wise he'll try to spend it in a way 'at'll bring happiness for a long time to come. Ther's some fowk feeared 'at they con niver spend brass safely; they're allus freeten'd of loisin' it; but they've noa need, for if they spent it i' dooin' gooid, they'll allus be sure o' gooid interest, for they'll be pleased every time they think on it. Nah, ther's some things i' this world 'at yo connot looise. It's a varry easy thing to loise a cork aat ov a bottle, but it's impossible to loise th' hoil aat ov a bottle neck. Yo may braik th' bottle all to pieces, but th' hoil is somewhear; it nobbut wants another bit o' glass twistin' raand it, an' yo'll find it's as gooid as iver it wor, an' it's just soa wi' a gooid action; yo may loise th' seet on it, but it's somewhear abaat; it nobbut wants circumstances twistin' raand it, an' yo'll find it's thear—it's niver lost. If fowk 'ud get into this way o' thinkin', ther'd be a deal moor gooid done nor ther is. Haiver mich brass a chap has, if he's moor wants nor he con satisfy, he's poor enuff; an' aw think if fowk 'ud spend a bit less time i' tryin' to get rich, an' a bit moor i' tryin' to lessen ther wants, they'd be moor comfortable bi th' hauf. But yo' may carry things too far even i' savin'. Aw once knew a chap 'at wor a regular skinflint; he'd gie nowt — noa, net as mich as a crumb to a burd; an' if iver any wor seen abaat his haase they used to be sat daan to be young ens 'at hadn't le'nt wit. Well, he once went to buy a seck o' coils, an' to be able to get 'em cheaper he fetched 'em throo th' pit; it wor th' depth o' winter, but as he had to hug 'em two mile it made th' sweeat roll off him.. When he gate hooam he put 'em daan an' shook his heead. "By gow," he sed, "awm ommost done, but aw'll mak' yo' pay for this, for aw willn't burn another coil this winter." An' he stuck, to his word, an' wheniver he wor starved, he used to get th' seck o' coils ov his back an' walk raand th' haase till he gat warm agean — an' he says they're likely to fit him his bit o' rime aat. "Well," yo'n say, "that chap wor a fooil," an' aw think soa misen, an' varry likely if he'd seen us do some things he'd think we wor fooils. We dooant allus see things i'th' same leet — for instance, a pompus chap wor once tawkin' to me abaat his father. "My father," he said, "was a carver and gilder, an' he once carved a calf so naturally that you would fancy you could hear it bleat." "Well, aw didn't know thi father," aw sed, "but aw know thi mother once cauved one, for aw've heeard it bleat." Yo' should just ha' seen him when aw sed soa! — didn't he pull th' blinds daan, crickey!

Progress.

This is the age of progress; and it is not slo progress nawther. The worst on it is, we're all forced to go on whether we like it or net, for if we stand still a minit, ther's somedy traidin' ov us heels, an' unless we move on they'll walk ovver us, an' then when we see them ommost at top o'th' hill, we shall find us sen grubbin' i'th' muck at th' bottom. A chap mun have his wits abaat him at this day or else he'll sooin' be left behund. Ther's some absent minded fowk think they get on varry weel i'th' owd way an' they're quite content, but its nobbut becoss they're too absent minded to see ha mich better they mud ha done if they'd wakken'd up a bit sooiner. Aw once knew a varry absent minded chap; he wur allus dooin' some sooart o' wrang heeaded tricks. Aw' remember once we'd booath to sleep i' one bed, an aw gate in fust, an' when aw luk'd to see if he wor commin', aw'm blow'd! if he hadn't put his cloas into bed an hung hissen ovver th' cheer back. Awm sure aw connot tell where all this marchin' is likely to lead us to at last, but aw hooap we shall be all reight, for aw do think ther's plenty o' room to mend even yet, but the deuce on it is,' ther's soa monny different notions abaat what is reight wol aw'm flamigaster'd amang it. Some say drink is the beset-ting sin; another says 'bacca is man's ruination. One says we're all goin' to the devil becoss we goa to church, an' another says we'st niver goa to heaven if we goa to th' chapel, but aw dooant let ony o' them things bother me. 'At ther is a deeal o' sin i'th' world aw doo-ant deny, an', aw think ther is one 'at just bears th' same relation to other sins as a split ring bears to a bunch o' keys; it's one 'at all t'oth-er things on: an' that's *selfishness*, an we've all sadly too mich o' that. We follow that "number one" doctrine sadly too mich, — iverybody seems bent o' gettin, but ther's varry few think o' givin' — (unless its advice, ther's any on 'em ready enuff to give that; but if advice wor stuff 'at they could buy potatoes wi', ther' wodn't be as mich o' that knockin' abaat for nowt as ther' is).

We're all varry apt to know the messur o' ivrybody's heead but us own; we can tell when a cap fits them directly, but we con niver tell when ther's one 'at just fits us. Miss Parsnip said last Sunday, when shoo'd been to th' chapel, "at shoo wondered ha Mrs. Cauliflaar could fashion to hold her heead up, for shoo niver heeard a praicher hit onybody harder in all her life," An' Mrs. Cauliflaar tell'd me "'at if shoo wor Miss Parsnip shoo'd niver put her heead i' that chapel ageean, for iverybody knew 'at he meant her' when he wor tawkin' abaat backbitin'." An'soa it is; we luk at other fowk's faults through th' thin end o' th' spy glass, but when we want to look at us own, we turn it raand.

"O, wad some power the giftie gie us
To see oursels as others see us,
It wad fra many a blunder free us
An' foolish notion.
What airs in dress an' g'ait wad lea' us
An' ev'n devotion."

Selfishness may do varry weel for this world, but we should re-member it isn't th gooid one does to hissen 'at he gets rewarded for after — it's th' gooid he does to others, an' although we may be able to mak' a spreead here, wi' fine clooas, fine haases, an' sich like; unless we put selfishness o' one side an' practise charity it'll be noa use then.

"For up above there's one 'at sees
Through th' heart o' every man;
An' he'll just find thee as tha dees,
Soa dee as well as t' con."

Try Again.

Look around and see the great men
Who have risen from the poor
Some are judges, some are statesmen,
Ther's a chance for you I'm sure.
Don't give in because you're weary,
Pleasure oft is bought by pain;
If unlucky, still be cheery,
Up and at it! *try again*

Jealousy.

It wad be a poor shop, wad this world, if it worn't for love! But even love has its drawbacks. If it worn't for love ther'd be noa jay-lussy — Shakspere calls jaylussy a green-eyed monster, an' it may be for owt aw know, an' aw dooan't think 'at them 'at entertain it have mich white i' theirs. If ther's owt aw think fooilish, it is for a hus-band an' wife to be jaylus o' one another; for it spoils all ther spooart, an' maks a lot for other fowk; an' aw'm allus a bit suspi-cious abaat 'em, for aw've fun it to be th' case 'at them 'at do reight thersens are allus th' last to believe owt wrang abaat others.

Aw once knew a chap 'at wor jaylus, an' his wife had a sore time wi' him. If shoo spake to her next-door neighbor, it wor ommost as mich as her life war worth, an' shoo wor forced to give ovver gooin' to th' chapel, becos if shoo luk'd at th' parson he used to nudge her wi' a hymn book. Th' neighbours pitied her, an' set him daan for a fooil; but he gate cured at last, an' aw'll tell ha.' Once he had to set off, an' as shoo worn't varry weel he couldn't tak her wi' him, but he gave her a lot o' directions afoor he went, an' tell'd her 'at he might be back ony minit. Well, if iver ther war a miserable chap it wor Jim, wol he wor away; but he coom back as sooin as he could, an' what should he see but a leet up stairs. His face went as white as chalk, an' he wor just creepin' to th' winder to harken, when a chap 'at knew him happened to pass. He knew how jaylus Jim war, soa he thowt he'd have a lark. "Halla, Jim!" he said, "coom here; aw've summat to tell thee. Tha munnot goa in yor haase just nah, for tha ar'nt wanted."

"What ammot aw wanted for, awst like to know?" said Jim.

"Well, keep cooil, an' aw'll tell thi. Tha knows tha's been away a day or two, an' aw think it's my duty to let thi know 'at last neet ther wor a young chap coom to yor haase to luk at thi mistress; an' shoo's niver been aat o; door sin', nor him nawther; an' my belief is they're in that room together just this minit."

"Aat o' my rooad!" sed Jim, "let me goa in If aw dooant pitch him aat a' that winder, neck an' crop, my name isn't Jim." Up stairs he flew. "Nah then, whear is he? whear is he?" he haw'led, an' seized hold o' th' pooaker.

"Aa, Jim," shoo sed, "Tha wodn't hurt th' child surelee?" an' shoo held up a bonny little lad abaat two days old, 'at stared at him as gaumless as gaumless could be, an' 'at had his father's nooas an' chin to nowt.

"By gingo, aw'm done this time!" said Jim, as he tuk it in his arms an' kust it. "Aa, what a fooil aw've been! tha'll forgie me, lass, weant ta?"

"Sure aw will, Jim," shoo sed. An' after that they lived happily together, as all dacent fowk should.

Winter.

Winter's comin'! Top coits an' nickerbockers begin to be sowt up. A chap enjoys his bed a bit better, an' doesn't like gettin' up in a mornin' quite as weel. Tawkin' abaat enjoyin' bed makes me think ova young chap aat o' Midgley at' gate wed an' browt his wife to Halifax to buy a bed, an' nowt wod suit her but a shut-up en, like her father an' mother had allus had: an' they wor't long befoor they fun a second-hand en, 'at they gate cheap, an' as they knew a chap 'at coam wi' a milk cart throo near whear they lived, they gate him to tak it hooam for 'em, an' it worn't long befoor th' beddin' an' all wor nicely arranged, an' they war snoozelin' under th' blankets. They hadn't been asleep long befoor he wakken'd wi a varry un-comfortabie feelin', but as his wife wor hard asleep he didn't like to disturb her. He roll'd o' one side an' then o'th' tother, an' rub'd his legs an' scratched his back, but he couldn't settle do what he wod. In a bit summat made him jump straight up ov an end, an' if he hadn't been dacently browt up, it's very likely he mud ha' sed some faal words, Wi' him jumpin' up soa sudden, th' wife wakken'd, an' jumpt up as weel, but as th' bed heead war abaat six inch lower nor that shoo'd bin used to, shoo hit her neet cap agean th' top an' fell back wi a reglar sass. "Whativer is ther to do, Sammy," shoo sed, as sooin as shoo could spaik, "strike a leet' wi ta!" Sammy gate a leet, an' blushed an ovver his face, for it wor th' fust time onybody had seen him dressed that way sin he wor a little lad. "Aw dooant know what ther is to do," he sed, "but aw cannot bide i' that bed, an' that's a fact." "What!" shoo says, "are ta ruein' o' thi bargain bi nah? but tha's no need to freat, for aw con spare thee at ony time." "Nay, Jenny," he sed, it's nooan thee 'at maks me uneasy, but aw fancy ther's summat wick i' that bed besides thee an' me.' "Is ther," shoo said, an' shoo flew off one side; "why whativer is it, thinks ta?" Sammy turned daan th' clooas, an' it just luk'd as if sombdy had been aitin' spice cake an' letten all th' currans drop aat. Tawk abaat fleas! They worn't fleas! they wor twice as big, an' they wor marchin' away like a rigiment o' sodgers. He stared wi' all th' een in his heead, an' shoo started a cryin'. "A'a, to think 'at aw should iver come to this, to be walked over wi' a lot o' pouse like that! What mun we do?" "Do! we mun catch 'em, aw expect," he sed, an' he began wi pickin' 'em off one bi one, an' droppin' 'em into some wa-ter 'at wor cloise by. "Well, mi mother tell'd me," he sed, "'at when fowk gate wed they began o' ther troubles; an' it's true an' all, but aw didn't expect owt like this, for if aw'd known, aw'd ha' seen th' weddin' far enough; aw did think 'at a chap wad be able to get a neet's rest anyway." "Tha can goa back to thi mother," shoo sed, "an' stop wi' her for owt aw care, an' aw wish tha'd niver left her, for aw'st get mi deeath o' cold wi' paddlin' abaat wi' nowt on; but does ta think tha's catched 'em all?" "Aw think soa, an' if tha's a mind we'll get to bed agean." "Nay, tha can goa to thi mother as tha freats soa," shoo sed. "Tak noa noatice o' what aw sed," sed Sammy, "tha knows aw wor put abaat a bit, an' it war all for th' sake o' thee." "Tha'll tell me owt," shoo sed, "put th' leet aat, an' let's see if we con get a bit o' gradely sleep." They gate into bed once more, an' shoo wor off to sleep in a minit, but Sammy wor rubbin' an' scrattin' hissen. "Wen, aw've heeard tell abaat things bein' ball proof and bomb proof, but aw niver knew 'at anybody wor bug proof befoor." Wi' him knockin' abaat soa mich shoo wakken'd agean. "Nay, Sammy," shoo sed, "aw'm reight fair stawld, it's all consait, aw'm sure it is." "Consait be hanged!" he bawled aat, "just feel at that blister an' then tell me if it's all consait." Nowt could keep awther on 'em 'i bed after that, an' they paraded abaat all th' neet like two gooasts, wait in' for th' cock crow. Mornin' did come at last, an' Sammy worn't long befoor' he had th' bed aatside. "What are ta baan to do wi' it nah?" ax'd his wife. "Aw'm baan to leave it wheal' it is wol neet," he sed, "an' if they havn't forgetten which road they coom, aw think ther's as monny as'll be able to tak it back to Halifax." Next neet they made a bed o'th' floor, an' slept like tops, an' next mornin' when they gate up, th' bed wor off. Whether th' cumpny 'at wor in it had taen it or net, Sammy couldn't tell, but he niver went to seek it. Fowk 'at buy second-hand beds, *tak warnin.*"

Persevere.

If you fail don't be downhearted,
Better times come by-and-by;
Soon you'll find all fears departed,
If you'll only boldly *try*
He who would climb up a mountain,
Must not sit him down and cry;
At the top you'll find the fountain,
And you'll reach it if you'll *try*

Though your comrades call it folly,
Persevere, you'll win the day;
Never let Dick, Tom, or Polly,
Stop you on your onward way,

There is always joy in striving,
Though you fix your goal so high;
Nearer every day arriving,
You may reach it if you *try*

Booith-Taan Election.

This place 'is nearly a mile from the good old town of Halifax.

Aa! ther wor a flare-up at Booith-Taan Hall that neet! It had been gein aat 'at they'd to be a meetin' held to elect a new Lord-Mayor, for New-Taan, Booith-Taan, an' th' Haley Hill, on which particular occashun, ale ud be supplied at Tuppence a pint upstairs. Ther wor a rare muster an' a gooid deeal o' argyfyin' tuk place abaat who shud be th' chearman. But one on 'em—a sly old fox—had kept standin' o' th' floor sidlin' abaat woll ivery other chear wor full, an' then after takkin a pinch o' snuff, he said, "Gentlemen, aw see noa reason aw shuddent tak this place mysen, as iverybody else has getten set daan." Two or three 'at wor his friends said "Hear, hear," an' two or three 'at worn't said "Sensashun!"

When iverybody's pint had getten fill'd, he blew his nooas, tuk another pinch o' snuff, an' stud ov his hind legs to oppen th' pro-ceedins. "Bergers and Bergeresses," he began, "aw've a varry un-pleasant duty to perform to-neet, which is, namely, to propooas 'at we have a fresh mayor," (Cries ov "Shame," "Gammon," "Th' mayor we have is ommost allus fresh!" (etsetra, etsetra etsetra.) "Gentle-men," he began agean, "what aw have to say is this,"—

"Luk sharp an get it said, then," said Stander, th' grocer.

"If tha doesn't hold thy noise, Stander, tha'll get noa moor snuff off me, aw con tell thi that; aw mayn't be as flaary a talker as thee, but what aw say is to'th' point, an' aw think 'at a constituency like Booith-Taan owt to be represented by somebody ov standin'."

"Better send th' chearman, he's stud den long enuft," said one.

"Prathi sit thi daan, if tha connot talk sense," said another.

"Its's time for sombdy to stand summat, for all th' pints is empty," said th' lanlord.

"Well, gentlemen," went on th' chearman, "th' question just dissolves itsel' into this: Who has it to be? Has it to be a Doctor sombdy, or a Professor sombdy, or a Squire sombdy, or has it to be a plain Maister?"

"Oh I let it be a Squire," said one. "E'ea, Squire Broadbent ul do," said another.

"Nah, lads, yo' 'Ie heeard th' chearman's resolushun, an' aw sit daan to call upon Mr. Stander, Esquire, grocer, to address yo."

Th' chearman doubled hissel' into th' shape ov his chear, an' after they'd gein ovver pawsin' th' table legs, an' knockin' pint pots, Stander gate up an' began.

"Fellow Municipallers (hear, hear), aw agree wi' what awr chearman says, 'at we owt to have sombdy o' standin' i' society to represent us for this subsequent year 'at's forthcomin'."

"Tha happen want's to get one o' thi own relations in," said Snittle.

"It ud seem thee better to keep thi maath shut, Snittle, till tha's paid me for yond Garman Yeast." — (Shame, shame.)

"Gentlemen, aw propooas 'at this meetin' dissolves itsel' into a depitation to visit Professor Holloway, to ax him if he'll represent us for th' next year. Aw dooant know him mysen, but we've all heeard tell on him, an' we've seen his pills an' ointment advertised, an' aw think he'd be a varry likely man to work awr business to th' best interest ov the whole communicants; an' noa daat he'd be able to heal up ony bits o' unpleasantness 'at's been caused wi' this election. Aw believe him to be a varry pushin' man, an' one ov a spyring natur; for as Elijah Barrett says (i' his book on leeanin' to blacksmith), 'One inch the heighest,' seems to be the motto he works on, for goa where yo will yo'll allus see one o' his bills a bit heigher nor onybody's else, an for that reason aw beg to propooas 'at he should be acceptted as a fit an' proper person.

The chearman stood up an' axed "ony chap to I say owt agean that 'at dar." Up jumped Billy Bartle, an' said, "Aw object to that in total; aw see noa reason to goa to Lunnon to find a mayor, soa long as we've professors at hooam, an aw propoosas 'at we ax —" ("Shut up! shut up!" "Ta' hold, an' sup." "Gooid lad, Billy,") etsetra, etsetra. etsetra.

Just then th' lanlord coom in an' turn'd off th' gas, for he said "they hadn't spent aboon eighteen pence all th' neet."

Th' chearman said he thowt they couldn't do better nor all have a pinch o' snuff wi' him, an' have a pint i'th' kitchen woll they talked things ovver; soa they went daan th' stairs, an' somha they managed to re-elect th' owd en afoor they went hooam, an' six on em hugged him o' ther heeads to th' top o' Ringby, an' niver heed if ther heeads didn't wark th' next mornin'.

Election.

Candidates at an election allus reminds me ov a lot o' bees turned aat, for they fly abaat th' country buzzin' an' hummin', wol yor fair capt what a din they con mak; but as sooin as they pop into th' hive o' St. Stephen's yo niver hear a muff—they're as quite as waxwark. Aw varrily believe 'at one hauf on 'em niver oppen the maath throo th' yaar end to year end, nobbut when they're sleepy, then they may gape a bit, but they do it as quiet as they can. As for them chaps 'at tawk soa mich befoor they goa, abaat passin' laws to give iverybody a paand a wick whether they work or laik, an' reducin' th' workin haars to three haars a day an' three days a wick: Why, its just gammon!

None think Alike.

What suits one body doesn't suit another. Aw niver knew two fowk 'at allus thowt alike; an' if yo iver heard a poor chap talkin' abaat somebdy 'ats weel off, he's sure to say 'at if he'd his brass he'd do different throo what they do.

Aw once heeard a chap say 'at if he'd as mich brass as Baron Rothschild he'd niver do owt but ait beef-steaks an' ride i' cabs. Well, lad, aw thowt, it's better tha hasn't it. We're all varry apt to find fault wi' things at we know varry little abaat, an' happen if we knew mooar we shud say less. Aw once heeard two lasses talkin', an' one on 'em war tellin' tother 'at sin shoo saw her befoor, shoo'd getten wed, an' had a child, an' buried it. "Why, whativer shall aw

live to hear? Aw didn't know 'at tha'd begun coortin'. Whoiver has
ta getten wed to?" "Oh, awve getten wed to a forriner, at comes
throo Staffordshur."

"Well, aw hooap, tha's done weel, lass; awm sure aw do. And
what does he do for a livin'?" "Why, its rayther a queer trade; but he
stails pots." "Stails pots, Betty! A'a aw wonder ha tha could bring
thisen daan to wed a chap o' that sooart. Aw'll keep single for iver,
woll awm green maald, afoor aw'll wed ony chap unless he gets his
livin' honestly." "Aw should like to meet ony body 'at says he
doesn't get his livin' honestly," says Betty; "nah thee mark that."
"Well, Betty, that maks noa difference to me; but aw say agean 'at
noa chap gets his livin' honestly 'at stails—noa matter whether he
stails pots or parkins." "Why, Nancy, aw thowt tha'd moor sense,
aw did for sure;— aw mean, his trade is to put stails on to pots."
"Oh! A'a! E'e! tha mun forgi' mi this time, Betty, aw see what tha
meeans; he puts hanels on to pots: that's it, isn't it." "E'ea." "Why, tha
sees, aw didn't understond." "Ther's monny a one has a deeal to say
abaat things 'at they dunnot understond, an' monny a one gets aw-
fully put aat wi' what sich like do say; but it isn't advisable to be soa
varry touchus at this day, an' as aw've read somwhear—

Time to me this truth has towt,
'Tis a truth 'at's worth revealin';
Moor offend for want o' thowt
Nor for any want o' feelin'.

An' aw believe that's true; but at th' same time it's as weel to be
careful net to offend onybody if we con help it, for a chap's fingers
luk a deeal nicer, an' moor agreeabler, when they're oppened aat to
shake hands wi yo, nor what they do when doubled up i'th' front o'
yor nooas. Soa yo see, yo connot be to careful o' yor words an'
deeds, if yo want to keep straight wi' fowk; an' it's a wise thing to be
at peeace. And if this is a unsettled time o' th' year, that's noa reason
'at yo should be unsettled. But as it isn't iverybody's lot to know ha
to get on smoothly, aw'll just give yo a bit o' advice; an' if yo learn
that, an' act on it, yo'll niver rue th' brass yo've spent, especially if yo
tak into consideration at th' profits are devoted to a charitable insti-
tution (that's awr haase).

If wisdom's ways you'd wisely seek,
Five things observe with care;
Of whom you speak, to whom you speak,
And how, and when, and where.

Seaside.

Iverybody 'at is owt is awther just settin' off or just gettin' back throo th' spaws. Ther's nowt like th' sea breeze! But a chum o' mine says th' sea breeze is a fooil to Saltaire, but he cannot mak me believe it. Ther's nowt ever suits me as weel at Blackpool as to see a lot o' cheap trippers 'at's just com'd for a day — they mean to enjoy thersen. Yo can see that as sooin as iver th' train claps 'em daan, away they steer to have a luk at th' watter. Ther's th' fayther comes th' furst, wi' th' youngest child in his arms, an' one or two rayther bigger poolin' 'at his coit laps, an' just behund is his owd lass, puffin' and blowin' like a steam engine, her face as red as a rising sun, an' a basket ov her arm big enuff for a oyster hawker. At one corner on it yo con see a black bottle neck peepin' aat. At th' side on her walks th' owdest lass; an' isn't shoo doin' it grand for owt shoo knows! Luk what fine ribbons shoo has flyin' daan her back, an' a brass ring ov her finger, varry near big enuff to mak a dog's collar on, an' a cotton parasol 'at luks ivery bit as weel as a silk 'un; and yo con see as shoo tosses her heead first to one side an then to tother, 'at shoo defies awther yo or onybody else to tell 'at shoo's nobbut a calico wayver when shoo's at hooam. But they get aside o'th' watter at last. "Ha! what a wopper!" says one o'th' lads, as a wave comes rollin' ovver. "A'a! but that's a gurter!" says another. Then th' father an' th' mother puts th' young uns all in a row, an' tell 'em all to luk at th' sea — as if ther wor owt else to luk at i' Blackpool. But yo may see at th' owd lass isn't comfortable, for shoo keeps peepin' into her basket, an' at last shoo says, "Joa — aw believe sombdy's had ther fooit i'th' basket, for th' pasty's brusscn, an th' pot wi' th' mustard in is brockken all to bits." "Neer heed, if that's all, its noa war for being mix'd a bit; it's all to goa into one shop." As sooin as owt to ait is mentioned, th' childer's hungry in a minit-even th' lass' at's been peraidin' abaat an' couldn't fashion to stand aside ov her brothers an' sisters coss they wor soa short o' manners — draws a bit nearer th' mother's elbow. Daan they sit like a owd hen an' her chickens, an' dooant they put it aat o'th' seet? It means nowt if th' mustard an' th' pickled onions have getten on th' apple pasty or potted mait an' presarved tairts squeezed all into one—they're noan nasty nice; an' then th' bottle's passed raand: cold tea flavored wi rum, an sweetened, wol th' childer can hardly leave lawse when they've once getten hold. An' wol they're enjoyin' thersen this way, th' owd chap's blowin' his bacca, an' tak's a pool ivery nah and then at a little bottle, abaat th' size ov a prayer book, 'at he hugs in his side pocket. After this they mun have a sail i' one o'th' booats, an' in they get, tumellin' one over t'other, an' bargain wi' th' chap for a *gooid* haar. Th' owd chap pools his watch aat an mak's sure o'th' time when they start, an' away they goa like a burd. "Isn't it grand?" says furst one an' then another. But in a bit th' owd chap puts his pipe aat an' tak's another pool at th' little bottle, an' his wife's face grows a deeal leeter coloured, an' shoo axes him ha' long they've to goa yet? Aat comes th' watch, an' they're capt to find 'at they've nobbut been fifteen minutes, an' th' owdest lass lains ovver th' side, an' after coughin' a time or two begins to feed th' fish, an' th' little uns come to lig ther heeads o' ther mother's knees, but shoo tells 'em to sit o'th' seeat, for shoo connot bide to be bothered; then shoo tak's a fancy to luk ovver th' edge, an' ther's another meal for th' fish. Th' owd chap's detarmined to stand it aat, soa he shuts his e'en, an screws up his maath wol it's hardly as big as a thripny bit—then his watch comes aat agean, an' he sighs to find they've nobbut been one hauf ther time. Th' chaps i'th' boat see ha' matters stand, an' bring' em back as sooin as they con. Aat they get, an' th' brass is paid withaat a word; but th' owd woman shakes her heead an' says, "Niver noa moor! It's a dear doo! Sixpence a piece, an' all th' potted mait an' th' apple pasty wasted."